THE SILVER ANNIVERSARY MURDER

By Lee Harris
(published by Fawcett Books)

THE SILVER ANNIVERSARY MURDER

A CHRISTINE BENNETT MYSTERY

LEE HARRIS

FAWCETT

BALLANTINE BOOKS • NEW YORK

The Silver Anniversary Murder is a work of fiction. Names, characters, places, and incidents are the products of the author's imagination or are used fictitiously. Any resemblance to actual events, locales, or persons, living or dead, is entirely coincidental.

A Fawcett Books Mass Market Original

Copyright © 2005 by Lee Harris

Published in the United States by Fawcett Books, an imprint of The Random House Publishing Group, a division of Random House, Inc., New York.

FAWCETT is a registered trademark and the Fawcett colophon is a trademark of Random House, Inc.

ISBN 0-449-00730-8

Cover illustration: Rick Lovell

Printed in the United States of America

www.ballantinebooks.com

OPM 9 8 7 6 5 4 3 2 1

In memory of Claire Smith,
my friend and agent for twenty-five years

Acknowledgment

With many thanks to James L. V. Wegman
for all his help

It was their Silver Wedding; such lots of silver presents, quite a show.

We must not grudge them their show of presents after twenty-five years of married life; it is the silver lining to their cloud.

—SAKI, *The Unbearable Bassington*

1

"Is this Christine Bennett Brooks?"

The voice in my ear was female, no-nonsense, and of indeterminate age. "Yes," I acknowledged. "Who's this?"

"Are you the one who solved the murder of that man in Oakwood last year?"

"Yes, I am."

"You've looked into several murders in the last years, haven't you?"

"Yes." If I sounded tentative, it was because I didn't know where this was going and I was somewhat intimidated both by the voice and by the direction of the words.

"Well, here's another one for you. A body will be found later today. I want you to be the first to know. I think you may enjoy looking into this death."

"Are you telling me someone has died?"

"I don't believe I said that."

My heart did something crazy. "Ma'am, is someone about to die?"

"I don't think I said that either."

"You—you aren't doing anything to harm yourself, are you?" I was trying to figure out how I could alert the police while keeping this woman on the line when I had only one telephone in my home.

"Let me repeat what I said, Mrs. Brooks: A body will be found later today. I'm not saying where it will be found or whose body it will be—whose body it is," she corrected herself.

"Who is this, please?"

"Mrs. Brooks, you are wasting your time and mine. I have things to do. I simply wanted to give you a heads-up, and you're making it very difficult for me. Today is my twenty-fifth wedding anniversary. I remember how happy—and beautiful—I was as a bride. I remember how handsome and strong and loving my fiancé was—my husband by the end of the day. Sadly, all things end."

"Please," I said, feeling panicky. "Don't do anything you'll regret. Don't—"

"I assure you I have no regrets. I just wanted to say thank you for listening to me and to tell you—" She stopped.

"Yes?" I said anxiously.

"And to tell you—Just a moment."

I thought I heard another voice and then the sound was muffled. "Hello?" I said. "Are you still there?"

There was a sound, loud and explosive. "Hello?" I said again.

The phone on the other end clattered to the floor or onto a table, and a few seconds later, as I shouted frantically into my phone, a dial tone pierced the silence. A chill passed through my body. Reverting to my oldest instincts, I crossed myself. Then, without hanging up, I put the phone down on the kitchen counter, grabbed my bag and keys, and ran out to the car.

"Just try to stay calm, Mrs. Brooks," the police officer said.

I had made for the Oakwood police station as fast as I dared. They knew me because Jack, my husband, is an NYPD detective lieutenant, and he has pals among the Oakwood police. I appreciated the uniformed officer trying to calm me, but it did no good. I was nearly in tears, less coherent than my usual fairly calm demeanor, and certain that I had witnessed a shooting over the phone.

"I'm fine. Please listen to me. Something terrible has just happened. Can you trace a call if the caller has hung up?"

"Possibly, but it depends on the circumstances. Would you start from the beginning and tell me what happened?"

I told him about the phone call, the female voice, as much of the conversation as I could recall. "And then there was another voice."

"On the phone?"

"No," I said with irritation, "There was another person on the woman's end of the call."

"Man or woman?"

"I think a man. I didn't hear anything clearly. But she stopped talking to me and started talking to him."

"And then?"

"And then," I said, swallowing, "there was an explosion— a gunshot, I think. And the phone fell. And then a dial tone came on the line."

"Sounds like a prank to me."

"Officer, please. She said a body would be found. I wasn't talking to a child. This was an adult woman. Oh yes, she said today was her wedding anniversary. Her twenty-fifth, I think she said. That would make her forty-five, give or take. I don't think this was a prank."

"We'll look into it."

I don't want to say he was lying to me, but I felt he was

placating me, not addressing me as an equal. "I left my phone off the hook," I said urgently. "Is there something you can do right now to find out where the call came from?"

"Oh, you did?" He sounded almost joyous. "Wait here a minute."

I stood in front of the classic high counter and watched him disappear into an adjoining room. I looked at my watch. At least fifteen minutes had elapsed since I put the phone down in my kitchen, since the gunshot rang in my ears. If someone was lying wounded in a house here in town, we could save him if we got there soon enough. Three long minutes passed. I was alone in the outer office of the Oakwood police station.

The phone rang, startling me. Someone inside must have picked it up as it stopped in the middle of the second ring. Come on, I thought. Do something.

The officer returned, a man in civilian clothes behind him. "This is Detective Palermo," the officer said. "Mrs. Brooks. Her husband is Lieutenant Brooks of the NYPD."

"A pleasure to meet you. I've met your husband. Jack, isn't it?"

"Yes. Will you try to trace the call?" I was in no mood for chitchat.

"Let's go back to your house and see what we can do. I'll follow."

I dashed out to my car, hoping he would move quickly. His car was parked closer to the building and he waited until I had turned into the street before he pulled out of his space. Less than five minutes later I was unlocking my front door.

"I just put it down without breaking the connection," I said, handing him the phone, which was making unpleasant noises.

"That was the right thing to do. You can dial a code to get the number of the last call made to this number. If you'd hung up and someone else had called while you were out, that's the number we'd get. This way we'll get the number of your strange caller."

I was relieved I had done the right thing. He took the phone, broke the connection, then turned it on again and dialed a few digits. He had taken a pen and a small notebook out of his pocket, and he wrote down a phone number as I watched. Then he dialed it.

He must have listened to twenty rings or more before he hung up. "Sorry," he said. "No one answers."

"Can you get an address?" I knew I was sounding pushy but I was certain that someone was lying dead or was dying in that house, and it was his job to find them.

"Give me a minute. Why don't you sit down and relax, Mrs. Brooks. We'll get to the bottom of this."

I was too keyed up to relax, whether sitting or standing. I walked away from him and stood at the entrance to our family room, looking away. He punched in a number, identified himself as a police detective, and asked for information on the number he had written down. It didn't take long.

"OK," he said, sounding more casual than I felt. "I've got an address. I'll be on my way and I'll let you know what happens."

"I hope you don't mind, but I'm going to follow you in my car. The woman who called said she knew who I was, but I didn't recognize the voice. I'd really like to know what's going on."

"Sure," he said, and we went out to our respective cars.

He knew where we were going; I didn't. I hadn't even asked if it was a great distance away. My son would be home from school in an hour and a half, and I had to be here or make a quick phone call to find someone to meet him. I kept the radio off in my car so I wouldn't be distracted and stayed close behind Detective Palermo. He signaled every turn so it was easy to keep him in sight.

I had been surprised when the officer introduced this man as a detective. Oakwood isn't a very big town, and I wasn't aware we even had detectives in the police department. It occurred to me that we might share his services with a neighboring town. Oakwood isn't the kind of community that has a homicide more often than once every several years, although there are occasional break-ins and young people have been known to get in trouble. It was hardly enough to keep a full-time detective busy, but it was comforting to know that someone with that kind of training was available when we needed him.

He stopped at the curb in front of a group of attractive garden apartments and got out of his car. I parked behind him and then joined him at a door.

"It's upstairs," he said. "Two B."

I followed him up and stood nearby while he rang the doorbell. When no one responded, he banged on the door.

"Looks like no one's home. Let's see if there's a neighbor."

The woman in 2A answered quickly, and Detective Palermo asked her about the occupants of the apartment across the hall.

She shrugged and looked unconcerned. She was an older woman, probably in her sixties, dressed in a cotton skirt and blouse, her hair half dark, half gray, and cut short. "The Mitchells. I haven't seen them for a while."

The name didn't ring a bell.

"You know where they are?" Detective Palermo asked.

"I'm not friendly with them. They complained about things, and I thought it was better to let them go their way and I would go mine."

"How many people live in their apartment?"

"I never see them come and go. More than one, I'm sure of that. A woman, maybe, I don't know, fifty. A man. Maybe two men. I guess they're a family."

The detective's slow pace was annoying me. I knew I shouldn't, but I butted in. "Excuse me, you said they complained about things. Did one of those people complain to you?"

"To me and the building manager."

"Which one complained to you?" I thought she might give us a description and it would ring a bell.

"The woman. Holly is her name, I think. It was a while ago."

"Can you give us a description?" Detective Palermo asked, finally doing his job.

"I told you, maybe fifty. Dark hair, thin, bracelets that jingled. Sometimes I would hear the jingle when I was inside, and I knew she was coming or going."

"Does she work?" I asked.

"Could be. She isn't around much during the day."

"You know her husband's name?" the detective asked.

"Ask the building manager. He's got that in his records."

"Thanks."

"Did you hear a loud noise there this afternoon?" I asked.

She shrugged again. "I just got home."

We went downstairs and found the manager, a man in his thirties named Larry Stone, at a desk in a small office. Detective Palermo asked if he could get inside the apartment to investigate a complaint made to the police about a possible crime.

"Sure," the manager said. He rose from his chair quickly, took a large ring of keys out of a file drawer, and led the way back to 2B. "What kind of crime?" he asked as we walked briskly up the stairs.

"We're not sure."

"You can look around. Just don't touch anything."

"You can stay and watch."

Larry Stone rang the bell twice before putting the key in the lock. In a second, he had the door open and he was inside. "Holy—" he said in amazement.

We followed him in and I realized the source of his surprise. The apartment was empty. There was no furniture, no pictures on the walls, no rugs on the hardwood floor.

"They moved out," he said. "What the hell's going on here?"

I wondered the same thing. "They didn't say anything to you?"

"Not a word. They got security coming. Why would they leave without getting it back?"

Detective Palermo walked into the kitchen. "There's a phone here," he called. "It's live."

I followed him. The phone was on the counter, a traditional instrument with a wire connected to a jack near the floor.

"Will you dust it for prints?" I asked.

He gave me a look I didn't appreciate. "I have no evidence of a crime."

"You have the report of a sane citizen," I retorted. "You know a call was made from this telephone to mine this afternoon. You know I didn't imagine it. Something's going on and I think it's a case for the police."

"OK, we'll check the phone for prints," he said.

I wondered if there was a way to get Det. Joe Fox, who worked for the county, to take over the case. He, at least, would believe my story. I had met him a couple of years ago, when he was as skeptical of me and my story as this man, but he has turned around, largely because I've helped him clear some local homicides. Maybe if Jack made a call . . .

"Do you mind if I look around?" I asked.

"Go ahead."

The apartment had three bedrooms, lots of windows and closets, two nice bathrooms, and well-kept hardwood floors in the living room and dining area. As I looked around, I couldn't help but wonder why a family would leave such a nice apartment without notifying the building manager, especially when they had a month's security waiting for them, something I would never do. And why would a woman return to this apartment to call me after having moved out?

Every closet was empty. The medicine chests were empty. If the lease read "broom clean," the occupants had fulfilled their obligation.

This was no ordinary three-bedroom apartment. It was extraordinary. The large kitchen had a beautiful tiled floor in a pale beige. Against the wall over the counters, just beneath the cabinets, were lights that illuminated the whole counter space. The wood of the cabinets may have been teak—I'm not an expert—and were finished in oil. They almost made my mouth water. The cabinets in my kitchen are older than I am and look it, although we had had them painted, which brightened them up.

The bathrooms were breathtaking, with marble fixtures that gleamed. Mirrors covered much of the wall, including a corner that reflected the background in infinity. I could only call it striking. Each bathroom had a large tub with spouts to shoot water at various levels, and two marble basins.

Whatever the occupants were paying for this apartment, it was a lot of money. They were not people who lived from hand to mouth or even a few steps above that. They were well-to-do and yet they had moved out without a word to anyone, as though they were behind on the rent.

There were phone jacks in all the bedrooms, but no instruments. Why had they neglected to remove the phone in the kitchen? What if she had called me from a different phone that had then been removed? I had no guarantee that her prints would be on the kitchen phone.

I went into the master bedroom last. It was large enough for a king-size bed and accompanying furniture. The master bath was shiny clean. I walked around the perimeter of the bedroom once again, finding the phone jack near a corner where the head of the bed would stand.

"Find anything?" It was Detective Palermo, who had taken a different route through the apartment.

"Nothing more than a little dust. Here's the phone jack." I pointed.

"Got one in every room." He knelt near the molding.

I turned to leave and noticed something on the carpet under the window. "What's this?" I asked.

Palermo took a look at it. "Hmm," he said.

"What does that mean?"

"It means it's a stain of some kind." He touched it. "Fresh, I'd say."

I felt apprehensive. "Any idea what it is?"

"If I had to guess, I'd say blood."

2

Jack and I talk a lot. The subjects we cover are many and varied. Eddie, our five-year-old, is a favorite topic. He is our only child, and like all the parents I know, we're trying to do a good job of bringing him up. Eddie's parents are not exactly two peas in a pod. Jack was a detective sergeant when I met him several years ago in the Sixty-fifth Precinct in Brooklyn about two weeks after I had been released from my vows as a Franciscan nun. He was going to law school at night, having earned his bachelor's degree the same way over a period of years. As a new wife, I learned not to expect him home until after ten in the evening nearly every month of the year.

As for me, I was educated by the nuns at the college affiliated with St. Stephen's, after which I got my master's degree in English elsewhere. My Aunt Margaret, with whom I was very close, especially after I was orphaned in my early teens, died several months before I left the convent, and her house became mine. I didn't think much about where I wanted to live; I just moved in and became a resident of Oakwood, New York, a pleasant, friendly community on the Long Island Sound, along the way to Connecticut. That house is still our home, although we have added a large section on the back that is a family

11

room downstairs and a master bedroom suite upstairs. Quite a difference from the cell I occupied in the Mother House for the second fifteen years of my life.

It was in that wonderful family room that we sipped coffee after Eddie went off to bed and talked about our day, our work, our problems, and all the other things that were part of our lives together.

"Let me get this straight," Jack said after I had retold my unnerving afternoon experience. "A woman called and you think she was shot while she was on the phone with you."

"Or she shot someone. Or someone nearby shot someone else. Yes, that's what I think."

"And this guy Palermo went over there with you."

"What do you think of him, Jack?"

"He's a guy waiting to collect a pension. Took some courses in fingerprinting and some other stuff and made detective. That'll give him a bigger pension. He's not full-time in Oakwood."

"I wondered."

"He's here, he's in the neighboring towns. He's no genius."

"Any chance Joe Fox can get involved in this?"

"I can call him and see if he's heard anything about it."

"I doubt he has. Palermo didn't seem very enthusiastic about investigating this."

"I'm not surprised. You didn't recognize the voice on the phone?"

"Not at all. But I've talked to so many people in the last few years, I could hardly remember all their voices. It was what she said when I answered the phone that was so strange. She knew my full name and that I had solved that murder on April first last year as well as other homicides, and she wanted me to know about this body that would be discovered later today."

"Lots of people know what you've done. It was in the papers." Most recently our local paper had written up my work on the homicide that occurred on April Fools' Day more than a year ago.

"It was as if she'd chosen me to look into . . . whatever was going on in that apartment. And I certainly have never been there before. I've never been to that group of buildings."

"You said Palermo thought there was blood in a bedroom."

"The master bedroom. I noticed some marks on the carpet as I was leaving, and he said they looked like blood to him."

"Let me tell you what's going to happen next. Palermo doesn't have much to go on besides that bloodstain, if that's what it is, but that would give his request for a crime scene technician to work up the apartment some weight. They'll do an in-apartment test first. Chemicals and black light will show the stain is blood, if it is. Then they'll remove the carpet, bag and tag it, and take it to the lab. If tests reveal that the stain is human blood, and if enough is recovered to do DNA testing, they'll match it if either a victim or a suspect turns up. They'll also vacuum the rug, look for hair in the bathrooms, and dust likely surfaces for prints, like tile, marble, glass . . . you get the picture."

"That should turn up a lot of useful information," I said.

"Did he seal the apartment when you left?"

"He said he would come back later with crime scene tape. I hope he did."

"Well, there's now a file on this, so Joe will have something to look at. He hasn't been over for a while, has he?"

"Quite some while."

"And he likes your coffee. Let's see what I can cook up."

The following day, Wednesday, I taught my morning class on mysteries by female American writers at a local college, stayed on campus through lunch, and came home to a free afternoon. My mother's dearest friend, Elsie Rivers, takes charge of Eddie on the day each week that I teach, an arrangement that suits all three of us. Eddie is in kindergarten this year, making lots of new friends and becoming very social. He goes to many more parties than Jack and I do and knows more about pop culture than I ever learned.

When I got home after lunch, carefully carrying a still-warm blueberry pie made by the food service department at the college, there was a message to call Jack.

"I talked to Joe Fox," Jack said, not wasting time on idle conversation.

"He know anything about what happened?"

"Nothing, but he's looking forward to coffee at our place tonight."

"Glad I picked up a blueberry pie."

"Hmm."

"What does that mean?"

"Do I really want to share it?"

"You really do. Remember the waistline."

"It's hard to forget. Like my wedding ring, it's always with me."

"Maybe I'll give him some to take home."

"Maybe you'll ask your husband first."

"See you later, honey."

I was glad Eddie came home with chocolate chip cookies from Elsie's. The cookies would satisfy all Eddie's sweet desires, and I wouldn't have to serve a pie that evening with a wedge taken out.

Det. Joe Fox showed up with a small bouquet of spring flowers, including a couple of pale pink tulips that made me smile with pleasure. He and Jack gabbed while I made the coffee and put the flowers in water. Joe was interested in Jack's work now that he had been a lieutenant for about a year. I listened to their conversation, thinking that cops talked a lot about their work, even when they weren't working.

"Mrs. Brooks," Joe said—he never calls me Chris—"it looks like you stayed up last night baking me a wonderful pie."

I explained about the great desserts the college sold in their dining hall. "And I'm prepared to add a dollop of vanilla ice cream," I offered.

"How can I resist?"

While we were sipping and eating, I told him of the events of yesterday.

"I called the Oakwood station and asked about it after Jack telephoned this morning," Joe said. "There isn't much paper on it, but they had the crime scene unit out this morning, and they confirmed the stain you noticed was blood."

"I was afraid of that."

"And I have the names of the people who rented the apartment—they haven't officially moved, you know—and we'll try to track them down. The building manager says their lease doesn't expire till fall, and they didn't notify him they were leaving."

"I wonder how they got their furniture out without anyone noticing. Or why they left."

Joe put a sheet of paper down in front of me with names

on it: Peter and Holly Mitchell. I shook my head. Mitchell hadn't rung a bell yesterday; Peter and Holly didn't help.

"I've asked myself the same questions," Joe said. "They cleaned the place out real good."

"Except for the phone in the kitchen. Maybe she left it there so she could call me."

"Or they could've had another phone in another room and took that with them after they made the call," Jack suggested, something I had considered myself.

"I'm not sure there was a 'they' after she hung up," I said.

"There's a good chance the call to you was set up in advance," Joe Fox said. "They could have moved out days ago and called from that apartment, knowing they couldn't be traced."

"But the bloodstain."

"Bloodstains don't necessarily mean foul play. I'll bet your little boy comes in with scraped knees and bloody knuckles."

I nodded.

"And all that's perfectly innocent." Joe took a chunk of pie and followed it up with ice cream, a dreamy look on his face.

"There was something else," I said. "I've been trying to remember. Something I noticed and forgot."

"The crime scene people will find whatever it was."

"It wasn't something I saw." I closed my eyes, trying to conjure up whatever had been tickling my brain all day.

"A sound?" Joe said. "Someone in another apartment? Crying, screaming, music? Maybe a smell."

"Yes! That's it, Joe. I smelled something. I forgot to mention it to Detective Palermo, and he may not have noticed it. It was cleaning fluid, a bleachy smell."

"Now, that's interesting," Joe said. "They were cleaning up. What room was that again?"

"The master bedroom. You don't use bleach in a bedroom. You use it in the kitchen and bathrooms. There was blood in that bedroom and someone tried to clean it up."

"You may have something. And by the time the crime scene folks arrived today, the smell may have dissipated."

"Yes," I said with satisfaction. "That's what happened. There was blood and they used bleach to get rid of it."

"They had to work pretty fast," Jack said. "Whoever was left alive in that room must have known you or the police would be on your way. Pressing star sixty-nine is commonly known, and people realize the police can find addresses when they have phone numbers to work with. The killer had to clean up and remove a body in broad daylight with maybe twenty, thirty minutes to do it."

"Unless it was staged." Joe looked thoughtful.

"Palermo said the stain was fresh," I said.

"We'll find out."

"Honestly, Jack, this one is too tough for me. The names Peter and Holly Mitchell mean nothing, the address means nothing. The fact that this woman knows I've worked on homicide investigations doesn't lead anywhere. I think I'll leave this to Joe and his squad."

Jack grinned. "Want to make a friendly little bet on whether you'll leave it to Joe?"

"Sure. How 'bout a dollar?"

Jack laughed. "My wife, the big spender. OK. I'll go for it." He pulled out his wallet and found a dollar bill.

I went to the kitchen and took a dollar out of my purse. Joe Fox was laughing. I handed my dollar to him. "You can hold on to the cash, Joe. We both trust you."

He pocketed the bills, shaking his head. "Well, now I'm

in a tough position. I won't be able to call on you for help, Mrs. Brooks."

"I don't know what you need help for. There's no body, no evidence of a crime, and no suspects. Your crime scene people will find a trace of blood, maybe some bleach, a little Windex on the windows. They'll analyze the DNA and find the person has no police record. And that will be that."

"That will be that," he repeated. "Until a body turns up. Then everything changes."

He was right about that. He promised to keep us informed, if there was anything to inform us about, and went on his way. I checked every phone book and file in the house for some reference to Peter or Holly Mitchell, with no luck. I called my friend Melanie Gross the next day and asked her if she recognized the names or if she knew any child in the school where she teaches named Mitchell. She checked the school files and turned up three Mitchells, but none lived in the garden apartments where Peter and Holly lived, and none had parents with those names.

Joe Fox called on Friday to say he had received the crime scene report. The stain was blood, and they would check the DNA and see if they could find a match in police files. I didn't expect them to. But I did want to know if the blood belonged to a man or a woman. I wanted to learn whether I had spoken to a killer or a victim.

Eventually, Joe called and said the DNA was from a male. As I expected, it didn't match with any DNA in police files that he could access. He reminded me that even though the person who lost the blood was male, it didn't mean the victim was male. The killer could have cut himself in the act of murder or in moving the body. It went without saying, however, that if the killer was female and of ordinary strength, she would have required assistance in moving the body. If there had been a body. If there had been a murder.

I went about the business of being a wife, mother, part-time teacher, and sometime word processor for my lawyer friend Arnold Gold. A week passed. I told the whole story to Mel as we walked the streets near our houses to get in shape for summer swimming and the bathing suits we would wear. Mel had made some calls to people in nearby towns, but no one had heard of the Mitchells. Even though I had said I wouldn't touch this case, I called the local churches to see if either of the Mitchells was a member or was known. Neither one was.

And that's where it stayed for about two weeks. My college course came to an end, and I took some books out of the library for summer reading to help me decide which to include in the fall course. Eddie's kindergarten went by bus to the Bronx Zoo in New York and I was one of the accompanying mothers. Joe Fox maintained his silence.

And then one late afternoon in June I got a phone call.

"Mrs. Brooks?"

"Yes."

"Detective Palermo, Oakwood PD. We met a couple of weeks ago."

"Yes, of course. I remember. Has something happened?"

"You might say so. We've found a body."

3

I had almost given up expecting such a call. The woman had said a body would be found that afternoon, and that afternoon was two weeks ago. It took me a moment to orient myself. "You think it's connected to the call I got from the Mitchell apartment?"

"We don't get a lot of bodies in this area, Mrs. Brooks."

"When was it found?"

"Yesterday. It's pretty deteriorated, as you can imagine."

"Then the person died some time ago."

"Looks like it. It's a female, by the way. Hard to tell from the body itself, but there's women's clothing on it and the size would fit a female. The autopsy is scheduled for this afternoon."

"I appreciate your call, Detective Palermo. Will you be working the case?" I was hoping for a negative answer.

"Probably not. I'm tied up with a lot of local stuff. I think the county'll take over. They have some good homicide detectives."

I smiled. "I'm sure they do."

"Someone'll let you know what's going on when we have more information."

I thanked him and hung up. The woman who had called

me had been killed. I was sure of that. Having spoken to her at such a crucial moment, the last one of her life, I felt a sense of sadness that I had been unable to save her.

I called Jack and told him the news. Joe Fox had not called him, so it was possible Palermo had not told him of the find. When I got off the phone, I called Joe myself.

"Mrs. Brooks, I have just heard some interesting news."

"So have I, Joe." I told him mine.

"About what I heard. It's a female, and from the condition of the body, she may well have died around the time you got your strange call. I doubt they'll be able to pinpoint the time of death, but they'll give us a range."

"Detective Palermo says he's tied up with local things. Does that mean you'll catch the case?"

"I've already talked to my lieutenant about this one. I think it'll be me."

"I'm glad to hear it. Will you keep me informed?"

"Of course. I'm sure there'll be news tomorrow."

He was prompt with his information. I was eating my tuna fish salad the next day and reading my *New York Times* when he called.

"It's a woman, as we guessed," he began. "Forty to fifty, maybe a bit more, about five-four, a hundred twenty to a hundred twenty-five pounds, dark brown hair starting to gray, good teeth and good dental work, no broken bones. She had her nails done shortly before she died."

I looked down at my own unmanicured hand as he said that. "You haven't told me how she died."

"Well, that's the neat part. There isn't a mark on her body. They'll do a tox screen, but that takes time. But it's a cinch she wasn't shot."

* * *

That was quite a punch line. I had fully expected him to
report on a gunshot wound, bullet, gun caliber, and all that
went with it. Instead, I had a puzzle.

I finished my lunch, drank the last of the tomato juice,
and sat myself down in the family room with the *Times*
and my quandary. Perhaps this woman had no connection
to the woman who called me. True, Palermo had said the
area didn't have many homicides, for which we were all
grateful, but it was always possible that the phone call had
indeed been a prank and that this body was an unhappy
coincidence.

The facts that I knew were so confusing and pointed in
so many directions that I could hardly use them as a starting point. It seemed to me someone had to canvass the
building the Mitchells lived in. At least one of them must
have held a job and owned some furniture, not to mention
a car. The thought of a car made me perk up. Jack could
easily check licenses and registrations. I went back to the
phone, thinking I had just forfeited a dollar. He would
laugh and tease me, but I wasn't going to stop thinking
because I'd lost a wager.

"Lieutenant Brooks."

His title still gives me a bit of a thrill. "Jack, I just talked
to Joe Fox."

"He faxed me his report a little while ago. I only
glanced at it, but it looks like a doozy. Nothing matches
anything we know—or thought we knew."

"The Mitchells must have owned a car."

"I'm sure that's occurred to Joe, but I'll get on it. Who
were they again? Peter and—"

"Holly."

"I'll have it with me when I come home. I don't want to
step on his toes, Chris."

"I understand."

"And I hate to see you lose a buck."

"Life is full of disappointments."

The way it worked out, after several phone calls, was that Joe Fox would do the good job he was trained to do and I would do the intuitive work that had helped catch a number of killers over the last half dozen years. Joe had already ordered a canvass and that would start tomorrow. Jack would find out what car the Mitchells drove, and Joe Fox would probably put out an alarm for it. By now, two weeks after the homicide, it could have been sold or driven out of state, but something might turn up. Mel and I had already tried the schools with no luck; I would have to mention that to Joe.

My hopes lay in the canvass. The Mitchells, or Mrs. Mitchell at least, must have had a neighbor that she was friendly with. And the building manager should know where one or both of them worked. They would surely have a bank account locally, and the police would find that. Those bits of information would provide something tangible to work with.

Later in the afternoon, Eddie and I walked down the block and across the street to the Grosses, and while Eddie played upstairs, Mel and I sat on her shaded patio and drank iced tea.

"The body turned up yesterday," I told her.

"Mrs. Mitchell?"

"A woman. Probably Mrs. Mitchell. The age is right for a woman celebrating twenty-five years of marriage."

"Too old to have kids in the schools."

"Maybe, maybe not, but it was a place to look. And they might have gone there a few years ago."

"It's very strange, Chris. Nobody I talked to had ever

heard of them. I think that if you asked five people in Oak-wood if they knew me, one or two would recognize my name."

"If she worked, she may not have had the kind of social life we have. She'd be too tired at night to go to council meetings and scream about injustice."

"Excuses, excuses," my friend said. "Something's fishy. Where did they find her body, by the way?"

"Mm. I forgot to ask and he didn't mention it. I'd call now but I don't want to be a bother. Joe Fox faxed his report, so maybe it's in that. Jack'll bring it home tonight."

"Sounds like you have your work cut out for you."

I explained about the friendly wager Jack and I had made.

Mel laughed. "Did you really think you would stay out of this?"

"What I really thought was that nothing would happen. The apartment was empty, the people had disappeared, the neighbor hadn't seen them. I thought we would find a body right away. When we didn't, I decided it was over. You know me well enough to know that I don't bet a dol-lar lightly."

"I know," Mel said. "But I'm glad you didn't stand on your principles and refuse to look into this. It's not just a homicide. There's other stuff going on."

"Mommy?" a young voice called.

"That sounds like mine." I got up and went inside.

"I wanna go home," Eddie said, looking unhappy.

"What's wrong?"

"I don't like Noah anymore."

"Did something happen?"

"He won't let me play with his new game."

"Maybe he's afraid it'll get broken, honey. Remember when you wouldn't let him play with a puzzle of yours?"

Eddie pouted. "I don't care. I wanna go home."

"Problem?" Mel said behind me.

"A very small one in the great scheme of things."

"Eddie, we have really good cookies out on the table. Want one?"

"Yes!" His eyes lit up, the slight fading in importance.

At that moment, a soft voice behind me said, "He can play with my new game, OK?"

"Sari, that's very nice of you." We worked out a settlement quickly, and Mel and I returned to the shady outdoors and our tea. "Whatever made me think bringing up a child would be easy?"

"Your innate trust in humankind, dear friend. And it won't be easy, but believe me, you'll be successful."

It's nice to have a friend who says the right thing at the right time.

Jack handed me the fax when he came home. I glanced at it but was too busy with dinner to look carefully. Later, I read it with a pencil in my hand. The body had been found near Oakwood Creek, a trickle of fresh water that meanders through town and attracts teenagers at night in the warm months and bird-watchers and hikers all year round. I'm not sure of its source but I suspect it empties into the Long Island Sound, which forms one of Oakwood's natural boundaries. The body had not been buried; instead, it had been covered with leaves and branches. A solitary hiker had literally stumbled on it and called the police on his cell phone.

"I've saved the best for last," Jack said, watching me make a few notes in my book.

I looked up. "There's more?"

"No car registered to either Holly or Peter Mitchell at that address."

That sounded impossible. While some people who live in Oakwood don't own cars, most of those are older people who have given up driving and rely on neighbors to do their shopping unless they live near one of the supermarkets. Occasionally I see an elderly woman with a wheeled wire cart filled with bags of groceries, walking cautiously along the side of a road. It always makes me nervous. "Mel's right; something's fishy."

"I'd check with the building manager, see if they paid by check or cash. Bet it's cash or a money order."

I had the same feeling. I looked at my watch. It was still early evening. "Let me call Marjorie Walsh and see if they're on the voting list."

"Want to make another bet?"

"I'm through betting for the rest of my life." I dialed Marjorie and spent a few minutes in the requisite chatter. Then I asked my question and waited while she went for the list.

"No Peter Mitchell," she said. "No Holly. If they're new in town, they may not have registered yet."

"They've lived here for some time, Marge. Well, not everyone votes."

"Right, although we get a good percentage in Oakwood. Better than a lot of the towns around us."

I didn't want to explain further so I thanked her and got off the phone.

"Not registered?" Jack said.

"Afraid not."

"Well, that's not unusual. I know a lot of guys on the job who stay away from the polls. Not that they don't care, they just don't want a record of affiliation. Let's see what happens in the canvass."

"And Joe will check if they forwarded their mail."

"And how they paid their bills. We'll turn them up." He sounded confident.

But I was starting to wonder.

The next morning, after Eddie went off to school, I drove to the creek, parked off the road, and walked down the mild slope to where crime scene tape had been spread over a sizable area, stretching from tree to tree and stake to stake where there were no trees. A lone local cop sat in his radio car, ostensibly guarding the scene. He was eating a bagel and drinking coffee from a thermos when I got there. I waved to him.

"Morning, Mrs. Brooks."

I didn't recognize him but I guess I'm better known than I think—always a surprise to a person who keeps to herself. "How long will you be here?" I asked.

He had opened the window. "Probably another day. They took a thousand pictures when the body was found, but we don't want the scene disturbed till we're sure we don't need any more."

"Where was she found?"

He put his bagel down on the seat, screwed on the top to the thermos, and got out of the car. I followed him to the yellow tape, which he lifted for me to go under. "About there." He pointed. "It's kind of sheltered with those bushes growing there. I can't let you walk any closer than where we're standing."

We were about ten feet from the area he had indicated, a leafy nest with bush branches bending over it. The killer must have raised them somewhat to get the body in snugly. "Do you know where her head was?"

"Left, I think, toward the water."

"Did you see her face at all?"

"Just for a second." He looked unhappy.

"Was she recognizable?"

"Not to me."

It wasn't the answer I wanted, but I didn't want to press him. There was no evidence I could see that a body had lain on that sheltered bit of ground. There were just leaves and brush, new green growth on the bushes. "Were there tire tracks?" I asked finally.

"You'd have to ask the crime scene detectives, ma'am. If she was dumped when she died a couple of weeks ago, it's unlikely they'd find tracks that were useful."

"Thanks, Officer Jennings." He had his name on a pin on the front of his uniform.

We walked back under the tape and I returned to my car, leaving him to his bagel and coffee.

Late in the afternoon, Joe called. "This is a real mystery, Mrs. Brooks," he began, "the kind that should delight you and drive me up the wall."

"What you're saying is nothing makes sense."

"Exactly. We canvassed the apartment building and came up with nothing. The Mitchells, if that's what their name was, kept to themselves and didn't get along with the woman across the hall, so no one can tell us anything useful."

"Did anyone see them move out?"

"One man thought he saw people loading an SUV with furniture two or three weeks ago. It's hard to pinpoint the time at this late date. But as you've heard, they didn't own a motor vehicle under either of their names."

"How did they pay their rent?"

"Cash. Does that surprise you?"

"Not at this point."

"But on time every month. And we've talked to a number of banks. There are no accounts in their names."

"So they weren't Peter and Holly Mitchell," I said. "They had other names, which they kept secret for their own reasons. Once a month they withdrew enough cash to pay their rent. They could have had credit cards in their real names, but no one in that complex would know what that is."

"That's the way I'm thinking."

"Joe, has a police artist made a sketch of the dead woman's face?"

"In fact he has. I just got it a few minutes ago. I'll fax it to Jack and you'll have it tonight. And we'll use it in our canvass."

"I'd like to try the nail establishments in the area. You said she'd had a fresh manicure when she died."

"Right. And I hear tell that women confide in their hair-dressers and manicurists, so maybe the victim let something slip."

If the victim was Holly Mitchell, I thought that was a long shot. These were careful people, but perhaps the desire to confide had overcome Holly's caution while she watched her nails redden. It was worth a try.

Jack came home with a couple of sketches, one of the face and one of the whole person. I laid them side by side on top of the *Times* in my lap and studied them. There were handwritten notes, too, that the eyes were brown, the height about five-four, the weight one hundred twenty to one hundred twenty-five. This was an estimate, as a fair amount of decomposition had occurred in the time the body had been secluded near the creek.

"Looks like you're drawing a blank," Jack said, putting down his sections of the *Times*.

"I don't think I've ever seen her before." I noticed the artist had drawn the full-length sketch with a skirt. She looked like a woman ready to go to work. All that was missing was her handbag and perhaps a fashionable briefcase.

"See what the nail places have to say."

"What if she worked in New York and had her nails done on her lunch hour?"

"Always possible. Then that's just bad luck. Let's not anticipate it."

He was right, but I was disappointed. Something in me had been sure I would recognize the woman, but she was a stranger to me, a stranger who was dead of mysterious causes, none of them a gunshot wound.

"You look troubled."

"I am. I wonder if this woman was even the one I talked to on the phone. I wonder if the sound I heard was a gunshot. I really wonder what this is all about."

Jack got up and went to the kitchen to get seconds of coffee. "Keep digging. Between the two of you, you'll come up with something."

4

My theory was that a woman trying to keep her identity a secret would not go to the nearest manicurist or hairdresser—or bank, for that matter. She would be in danger of having a neighbor walk in, recognize her, and want to chat. After I noted all the nail places in Oakwood and surrounding towns, I drew a map and plotted them, deciding to leave the nearest for last. I had a feeling the police would work in reverse, and if I was lucky, I would come up with something before they did.

On Saturday morning I left father and son to do their weekend thing together and set out to visit nail shops. The first one on the list was several miles from the apartment building where the fictitious Mitchells had lived. I explained my mission to the receptionist, a young woman with nails that were long and multicolored. I would have been afraid to shake hands with her.

She didn't recognize the face in the sketch but generously invited me to talk to the five manicurists, all of whom were hard at work. One after the other, they shook their heads. I took the opportunity to ask their clients as well, on the chance that one of them had seen Holly in another location or, better still, had known her personally. No luck.

This wasn't the first time I had made these kinds of inquiries, and I knew better than to feel defeated so early. I crossed off the name of the establishment and drove to the second on the list. The names themselves were inventive. Several called themselves some kind of spa. The one I was headed for was called Shimmer.

Shimmer it might, but no one there recognized Holly either.

Number three was Nails R Art. The mirrored front window prevented a view inside but an oval section in the door was transparent glass, facilitating safe entries and exits.

Inside, it was bustling. The receptionist wore a smock with women's hands painted on it, each set of nails done differently. Her own, by contrast, were covered with a colorless gloss. I rather liked it.

I introduced myself and showed her the sketch. She looked at it carefully, then focused again on me. "I haven't seen her for about a month."

"But you know her?"

"Oh yeah. She came in every week or two. She was Ronda's client." She pointed to her left. "That's Ronda over there."

"What's this woman's name?" I asked.

"Rosette something. Wait a minute." She turned back several pages of her appointment book. "Parker. Rosette Parker."

"Is she married?"

"I think so. Ronda would know. She sees her hands all the time."

"When will Ronda be free?"

She looked at her watch. "Five minutes. Tell her you

want to talk to her. She has a little time before her next appointment. There was a cancellation this morning."

Ronda confirmed she would be free soon and told me to sit and make myself comfortable. I did as she suggested, finding a new issue of *Time* magazine on the rack. I had hardly gone through the table of contents when Ronda called me to follow her. We went downstairs to a basement kitchen and break room. A small microwave sat on a counter near the refrigerator. All the comforts of home.

I explained what had happened without being too explicit. When I said a body had been found, Rondo drew in her breath and opened her eyes wide. I asked her to look at the sketch, and she quickly identified the face as belonging to Rosette Parker.

"How long has she been your client?" I asked.

"About two years. Maybe not that long. Could I look at that again?"

I handed her the sketch, which seemed to mesmerize her. "Was she married?"

"I'm pretty sure she was. She wore a thin diamond band on her left hand, very nice diamonds."

"Did she ever talk about her husband?"

"She never talked about anything personal. She was pleasant and she tipped well and we talked, but I never heard her say much about her private life."

"What about children?" I asked.

"I don't know. I guess I assumed she had them because she was married and the right age, but I don't think she ever mentioned them. She worked, I know that."

"Do you know where?"

"Uh, maybe White Plains." White Plains is a metropolitan center northeast of New York City, a great deal smaller than New York but the largest city in the area. It has department stores and the expected malls, buildings full of business offices, and too much traffic.

"Did you ever see her car?"

"I don't know. She parked outside but I can't say I ever—wait a minute. I think I once saw her get into a maroon SUV-type car."

That could be the one the Mitchells' neighbors had seen filled with furniture a few weeks ago. "I don't suppose you noticed a license plate," I said with no hope that she had.

She smiled. "Sorry. Uh, could I ask you something? When did Mrs. Parker die? The last time I saw her she seemed fine."

"She died a few weeks ago. When was the last time you saw her?"

She calculated. "Three weeks ago? Four? It'll be in the book at the desk."

"Did she tell you what kind of work she did?"

"I think it was something in public relations. She saw clients, I know that. Every so often she'd tell me a little story about one of them, something funny that happened. One woman locked her purse in her car along with the key, and Mrs. Parker gave her lunch money and called the police to help her break into her car."

"Did she ever recommend anyone to be your client?"

"Never. I'm sure of that."

I wasn't surprised. When you're using two names, you have to be very careful not to entangle your personas. "Was she a regular?"

"Pretty regular. Sometimes she had to go out of town and she couldn't come in."

"Does the shop have her phone number?"

"They must. We have to be able to call in case there's

bad weather and I can't get in or I'm sick or something like that. They should have it at the desk."

"Anything else you can tell me, Ronda?"

"She was a nice woman. I'm sorry she's dead. Now I know why she missed her last appointment."

We went back upstairs—it was almost time for Ronda's next appointment—and Ronda took the full-length sketch from me. At her station, she pulled over a bottle of bright pink polish, opened it, removed the excess liquid from the brush, and dabbed it over the fingertips on the sketch. They were hardly more than little circles, but they brightened up the otherwise black-and-white picture. She handed it to me carefully, screwed the cap back in the bottle, and pushed it to its accustomed space.

On my way out, I stopped at the desk and asked for the date of Mrs. Parker's last appointment and for her phone number. The phone number was on file in their computer; it was the same number as the phone in the apartment. That, at least, established the dead woman, whatever her name might have been, had lived in that apartment. The last time she'd seen Ronda was the day before I got the phone call. I headed home.

"Good work," Jack said.

"What kind of work did you do, Mommy?" Eddie asked. The two of them were preparing vegetables for our dinner. Jack takes over the cooking on weekends, mostly because he enjoys it but also, I'm sure, because the quality of what he cooks is so far superior to what I cook.

"It wasn't really work, honey. I was looking for someone and I found her. Can I have a carrot stick?"

He handed me one and I crunched it. "Mm. This is sweet."

"Daddy is going to play baseball with me after lunch."

"I guess it's that season. Don't break any windows, you guys."

Eddie laughed. I wasn't sure what was so funny.

Jack called Joe Fox after lunch, and when he was sure Joe didn't mind being bothered on a Saturday, he gave me the phone.

"I found the manicurist," I said.

"Well, you're one giant step ahead of my cops. They reported that they've covered all the ones in Oakwood and have branched out to neighboring towns."

I told him I had started with neighboring towns and why.

"Good thinking. What do you have?"

I gave it to him quickly, ending with the phone number.

"So the victim lived there. And she must have had a husband or significant other because the building manager had his name and probably his signature on the lease. But who knows what name they kept their money under. And where's the husband?"

"I had to leave a few things for you, Joe," I said.

"Right. If you show us up, there'll be hell to pay. Well, the ME was able to lift fingerprints from the body. We'll be able to compare them with those we found in the apartment. I guess we'd better look for an account for Rosette Parker in the local banks, not that we have any reason to believe she stopped with two names. Anyway, it's too late today. We'll have to wait for Monday. But you've made a good start, Mrs. Brooks. If you're looking for a job, I'll be glad to recommend you to the county."

I admit to feeling flattered. I filled in what I had left out initially, that Ronda thought Rosette might have worked in White Plains, that she said nothing about her family but wore a diamond ring that could have been a wedding band.

"Sounds like Holly/Rosette was a careful person. When we have the prints, we'll see if she has a record."

"And a name she was born with."

"That, too. I'd especially like to know if there's a family, either on her side or her husband's. And it would be nice to know where he disappeared to."

"A lot of things we don't know," I said. "I'll follow my intuition, Joe, and try to keep from getting underfoot."

"So far that's not a problem. I have to say, though, I didn't expect you to lose that dollar quite so fast."

"Nor did I." It still rankled a bit. "Any labels in her clothes, Joe?"

"Brand names but no store labels. I'm told the labels are in the more-than-moderate range. Someone in that family must have made money—and they must have kept it somewhere. Tell me again about the last appointment with the manicurist. You said that was the day before the woman called you?"

"Yes. Rosette had a morning appointment. The woman called me the next day in the afternoon, a little after lunch, I think. Palermo should have that in the file."

"He should. You're right." I wasn't sure whether he was being sarcastic or merely stating a fact. "Finding them through the bank isn't going to be easy. With ATMs, people can withdraw and deposit money without personal contact except for the first time, when they open the account. And who'll remember them from years ago?"

"But don't you think they'd have had to use Mitchell as their name? The statements had to be sent to their apartment, and it was rented under that name."

"Could've used a box number."

"I hadn't thought of that."

"And we still don't know if she's the woman who called you, Mrs. Brooks. Just because she lived in that apartment doesn't mean she made the call."

"Well, I guess there should be blood work coming in soon. That may answer some questions."

"There will, and I will share it with you. Don't give up while you're getting results."

I left it there for the weekend but I didn't stop thinking about it. I've found that even when I'm not actively involved, my mind keeps working and tosses me ideas when I least expect them. We now knew that Holly Mitchell and Rosette Parker were the same person, but that would only be useful if we could find other places where those names had been used. It certainly sounded as though Holly/Rosette was keeping a low profile, but I couldn't imagine why. What I thought of was the complications of collecting insurance and eventually Social Security without a consistent name. If Holly worked for ten years and Rosette worked for another ten, that didn't add up to twenty years of benefits. And if she had a job and wore fairly expensive clothes, a lot of people had to know her under one name. She had to have picture ID to fly to business meetings, although I assumed an old driver's license would suffice. It had for me before I acquired my first passport last year to take the trip to Israel when Jack got a two-week assignment in Jerusalem.

Joe Fox had mentioned that the victim might have a record, which they would discover when her fingerprints were run. That could account for her not wanting employers and landlords to know her real name. Of course, it might have been her husband who had been incarcerated, and we knew nothing about him. It was dizzying.

But other explanations could account for her use of several personas. Topping my list was the possibility that she was hiding from someone, running away from someone who was hunting for her. One hears frequently about the government giving mobsters and their families new identities and homes in locations distant from their original homes. Were Rosette and her husband in that situation? Again, the fingerprints should provide an answer, unless the files were sealed even to the police.

I was starting to think she could not possibly have children. I couldn't imagine raising a child who went to school with one name and took piano lessons with another. Thinking about this became exhausting, and I was glad I would have Sunday off to think about other, pleasanter things.

My cousin Gene, who is mentally retarded, lives in a home for adults. When my aunt was alive, she had to get herself to the neighboring town to visit him, a difficult task after my uncle died, as she never learned to drive. But when I moved into her house a few months after her death, Greenwillow, the residence, also moved to Oakwood. I am a frequent visitor there, often with Eddie, who plays with Gene as though they are equals. Gene is very gentle with Eddie and I know they love each other. The day may come when Gene is in Eddie's care, and I want their relationship to remain solid and close.

On that Sunday, all four of us attended mass together and then Gene came home with us for Sunday dinner. In the afternoon we all played baseball in the backyard. I'm never very clear on the rules of the game or how many teams we are, so I let Jack take care of that part. Then we drove Gene back to Greenwillow.

It was a tiring day, and Eddie went to bed early, keeping the baseball mitt on his night table the way I used to keep a favorite doll near me when I slept. Gender really seems to mean something, even early in life.

"Joe Fox thinks this woman, the victim, might have a record," I said to Jack when we were alone in the family room.

"Sounds like you don't."

"I don't rule it out, but I think she could have been hiding from someone, someone who wanted to kill her."

"You could both be right. Someone did kill her, after all."

"What I mean is, she may not have been hiding her past, just trying to hide herself from someone who had a grudge or who wanted something from her."

"It's as good a theory as any. Either you or Joe will have to find out more about her so as to trace back to whatever she was hiding from. The fresh manicure was a good lead. It would be nice if you could find a friend."

"Or an employer. She might have given her high school or college credentials to get the job, or the names of other companies she worked for."

"I hate to tell you that employers don't do much checking."

"There has to be something, Jack. We live in such a technologically sophisticated age that I can't believe a person can shop and take care of a car and yet live so easily with an assumed identity even if she paid for everything in cash."

"Which is a good assumption."

"But what about the pharmacy? Even if you're healthy, as I am, my dentist occasionally prescribes an antibiotic for me."

"And a prescription presupposes a dentist or a doctor."

"Who will know you by whatever name you give him the first day you go. I'm trying to remember if the dentist required my Social Security number."

"Suppose you gave it to him. If this Holly/Rosette woman wrote down nine digits, what are the chances the doctor, the dentist, the pharmacist, or even a surgeon checked them out, especially if she said she had no medical insurance and would pay her bill in cash?"

"No chance," I agreed. "So here we are in a society that tracks you in and out of stores, offices, hospitals, and whatever, and we can get away with using a fraudulent name and ID number and no one knows. It seems paradoxical."

"It may be, but it works—that is, until a cop hauls you over for speeding and finds a bunch of inconsistencies."

"I'm going to have a go at pharmacies tomorrow. Hopefully, someone will recognize Holly/Rosette's picture and tell me she took an unusual medication for a rare condition."

"And everything about her life is documented including the names of her parents, her children, and all her siblings."

"Wouldn't that be wonderful?"

"Dream on, honey. And good luck. I'm sure Joe Fox will give you double flowers if you pull that off."

5

I daydreamed that Holly/Rosette Whatever might use a different name everywhere she went. After canvassing pharmacies and banks, hair salons and department stores, I might accumulate twenty or thirty names attached to her picture. But I decided not to worry about that unlikely situation. I got Eddie off to school, nearly his last week, and put my notebook in my bag. As I was getting ready to leave, the phone rang.

"Hope I haven't bothered you, Mrs. Brooks." It was Joe Fox.

"Not at all. Have you something to tell me?"

"You know they've been doing DNA analysis on the blood in the apartment and the tissue of the body."

"Yes."

"So far we haven't gotten a match on the body's prints or on the blood."

"Which means no records."

"Right. Not so far. My people are out there visiting banks and stores near where she lived."

"She didn't bank where she lived and she didn't shop where she lived." It seemed such a waste of time to me. "This is a woman who's trying to keep a low profile. She's not going to walk into supermarkets where a neighbor who knows her as Holly or Mrs. Mitchell might run into her and make small talk that could compromise her."

"You could be right—you've been right before—but this is the way we generally do it. Dare I ask what you're up to this bright Monday morning?"

"I'm checking pharmacies," I admitted.

"And none of them will be near the apartment complex."

"Not unless I fail farther away."

"I'd put my money on your not failing, but please keep me in your loop."

"My loop," I repeated, smiling. "My very little loop. You and me, Joe. Without you in it, it's a straight line going nowhere."

"That'll be the day."

There is nothing more boring than basic detective work. Ask the same questions to fifty different faces and hope one lights up. And then ask more questions. I did this the way I'd done the manicurists on Saturday, checking the yellow pages, sketching a map, driving to the most distant location first. Once again, I thought she might do her drug and cosmetic shopping where she worked, but since that wasn't confirmed, this was all I had to go on.

It would be nice to say that I dropped into the right drugstore first, but it didn't happen that way. I dragged myself from one to another, often showing the picture to several people, as some of the chain pharmacies have many pharmacists working for them—and there was always the chance that the one I wanted was off on Mondays. I presented the picture and gave everyone the two names I had. Some looked at the face intently, which I appreciated; others gave it a cursory glance and turned away with a bored expression. No one recognized her.

I had drawn a semicircle several miles deep for my canvassing area. It was a semicircle and not a full circle because Oakwood is on the Long Island Sound, not that this made my task any easier; I just increased the distance from the center to the farthest drugstore. A lot of heads shook; no one identified her.

I stopped for lunch at a restaurant I sometimes take Eddie to, looking at my list as I ate, counting the places that didn't have check marks next to them. The cops, I thought, had probably found the right one in the first ten minutes of their search, a hundred yards outside the garden apartments, all my theories shot. I sipped iced coffee and thought about what to do. Maybe it wasn't too late to retrieve the dollar I'd bet.

I finally decided to check out a privately owned drugstore in the same little strip mall where I'd eaten, even though it was one of the last pharmacies on my list. It was in Oakwood, but it was more than a mile from the Mitchell residence. I went to the counter at the back of the store and asked the young man if he knew the woman in the pictures.

"The cops were here this morning with the same picture," he said.

"And?"

"And I told them I didn't know her."

"Did they ask anyone else who works in the store?"

"Mr. Greeves was out when they came in."

"Is he here now?" It felt like pulling teeth.

"Yeah. Wait a minute."

I knew Mr. Greeves slightly. When we married, Jack insisted we open an account here. I always resist such ideas, wanting to pay as I go, but he pointed out that medication could be expensive. I found out how right he was the first time Eddie got sick as a baby—and I didn't have enough in my purse to pay for medicine that I needed right away.

"Mrs. Brooks, how are you?" Mr. Greeves is a big, graying, friendly man and a lifelong pharmacist. I'm told his father owned this business before him.

"In good health," I responded. "I wonder if you recognize this woman."

I handed him the sketch of her face. His forehead tightened as he pored over it. He jutted his lower lip out. "I don't know," he said.

I gave him the full-length sketch and watched a slow smile appear. "You know her?"

"She came in maybe a month ago. No one was at the counter so I waited on her myself. It's the fingernails that made me remember. They were so bright and fresh and such a pretty pink. I said something about it and she kind of blushed."

I felt hope rise within me. "Did she have an account with you?"

"I'm not sure she was ever in here before that day or after."

"Did she ask you to fill a prescription?" I asked, almost crossing my fingers.

"No, nothing like that. She took a couple of items off the shelf and paid cash. That's when I noticed her nails. And she was dressed like that, in a suit, very business-like."

"I don't suppose she gave you her name."

"No reason to. It was a cash transaction. But that's her. I'd bet on it."

That was as far as it went. She had simply been a woman off the street picking up a few necessities. Well, I thought, at least I had gone one small step beyond the police.

I went back to my list, determined now to show both pictures to everybody. You never know what will trigger a memory.

Elsie was picking up Eddie at school so I didn't have a deadline. It's amazing how many pharmacies were in this group of towns. It made me wonder how people picked only one for themselves. Mr. Greeves's store delivers, and that had been our main criterion—that and the charge account.

I grew weary and bleary-eyed, not to mention tired of hearing people say no. It occurred to me as I walked into what would surely be the last drugstore I would visit today that I should buy some Band-Aids for the bathroom upstairs that Eddie uses. I took a good-size box off the shelf and walked up to the counter, waiting behind an old woman with a cane. The cashier handed her two prescriptions in a paper bag, and the woman gave her name for them to charge the purchase.

I put my box on the counter.

"Anything else?" The cashier was a middle-aged woman who looked vaguely familiar. I thought she might live in Oakwood.

"I wonder if you recognize this woman." I laid the pictures on the counter and took out my wallet to pay.

"She comes in a lot."

"She does?"

"Yes. I haven't seen her for a while, but I was away on vacation, so I might have missed her."

"Do you know her name?"

"I don't think she has an account with us. She pays in cash. I always have to make change from a fifty."

"Does she bring in prescriptions?"

"I don't know. Let me ask the pharmacist." She went behind the high counter where the pharmacists worked and showed the pictures around.

Before she came back, a woman's voice behind me said, "I know her. You looking for her?"

I turned to see the old woman with the cane. "I'm looking for people who know her."

"That's Rosette Parker. She picks me up sometimes in the morning and takes me to the bus stop. It's very nice of her but it's so much trouble getting into that SUV of hers, sometimes I wish she'd just go by and let me walk."

I smiled with sympathy. "When was the last time you saw her?"

"Quite some time ago. Weeks. But the weather's been nice."

"Ma'am?"

The woman behind the counter was back. The pharmacists didn't recognize the pictures, she said. I thanked her and turned back to my new informant. "May I take you somewhere?" I offered.

"Just home. If you don't own a van or a pickup." She laughed.

I assured her I drove a small car and that she could get in and out of it easily. Outside she told me the cane was more for reassurance than physical necessity. She had had a hip replacement and was doing very well.

We talked while I drove the short distance. "She told me her name and I told her mine, maybe the second or third time she picked me up. I'm Gladys French, by the way. Pleased to meet you."

"Christine Bennett. Go on. I'd like to know everything you know about her. Was her husband ever in the car when she picked you up?"

"He was usually there, but she always drove. I think she dropped him off where he could get a ride or a train into the city. I got off first, so I don't know."

"What was he like?"

"I don't know what you mean by that," Gladys French said. "He was a man. He sat in the back, which was funny, and read the paper. Sometimes he'd say, 'IBM was up a point, hon.' Or 'That damn GE was down again, hon.' He always called her hon."

"Do you know where he worked?"

"Haven't the faintest. But I'm pretty sure they didn't work in the same place. That's why she was driving, so she could drop him off and go on her way."

"Did she ever tell you where she worked or what she did?"

"Not that I recall. Pull into the next driveway."

The house was white with turquoise trim, a doll's house with lush plantings and a charming dogwood tree in front. I drove up to the one-car garage and turned off the motor, expecting to help her to the front door, or at least ready to offer to do so.

"Come inside. We'll have a cup of tea."

I looked at my watch. I couldn't leave Eddie forever and I had dinner to cook.

"Oh, don't look at the time. Come in for fifteen minutes. We'll sit and have a nice cup of tea and you'll be on your way."

"That sounds like fun." I got out and opened the door for her.

She was steady on her feet, even without using the cane,

which hung on her left arm. She opened her front door, and we went inside to a living room filled with fine old furniture and a beautiful Oriental rug.

"Come in the kitchen with me and we'll talk while I boil the water."

I followed her and took down the cups and saucers at her bidding. They were the kind of fine china my aunt always used.

"What's your interest in Rosette?" she asked. "I've been answering a lot of questions but I don't know what you're after."

"She died, Gladys," I said.

"No." She turned from the stove to look at me, shock on her face. "A young woman like that? She couldn't have been more than fifty." Then she said, "That's why I haven't seen her these last weeks, isn't it?"

"She died about a month ago. There's reason to believe she was murdered."

Glady drew in her breath. "Murdered!"

"Her body was just found last week. But she was missing for a while."

"Oh my goodness." She pulled a chair away from the small table and plopped into it. "Excuse me. Just hearing that made me feel dizzy. It's all right." She raised her hand to keep me away. "I'm fine. Poor thing. And who are you then? Her daughter?"

"I'm a stranger who got involved in a complicated way. The police are looking into her death and I thought I'd try to find out what I could for myself. It was just luck I ran into you in the pharmacy."

"Well, with my prescriptions, you could run into me there almost any day of the week. How did she die?"

"They don't know yet. They're checking for drugs and poisons and things like that."

"She didn't do drugs."

"I'm sure she didn't. But she may have been given something. We'll find out when the lab work is done. Can you talk now?"

"Have I stopped talking?" She smiled and then jumped up as the teakettle began to whistle. "Go ahead, ask your questions. We'll just let the tea steep a minute if it's all the same to you."

"It's fine."

We sat at the table. Before each of us was a cup with an inverted saucer over it and a string and tag hanging over the side. After a couple of silent minutes, Gladys put her saucer under the cup, squeezed the tea bag by wrapping the string around it and a spoon, and then took a little sugar with a dry spoon. She pushed the sugar pot toward me, but I chose a slice of lemon instead.

"Did you ever notice Rosette's license plate number?" I asked, doubting that she had.

"Well, you know, it's not the sort of thing I ever look at, but hers had three Bs in a row, so when I heard a honk and turned around and saw the Bs, I knew it was Rosette."

"That's very helpful, Gladys. I think the police will be able to find the vehicle with that information."

"Why don't they just look up her name?"

I realized I'd gotten myself in a corner. "She may have used more than one name."

"No. Why would she do that?"

"Nobody seems to know. Did she call her husband by name?"

"Let me think." She sipped, then sipped again. "Not that

I recall. And he only called her hon. I thought that was cute."

"So do I. Tell me, did she ever say where she was going those mornings she picked you up? Work? A particular place?"

"She could've said White Plains. I think she did once. Oh yes, there was one other thing. On the seat where I sat or on the floor on the side where I sat there was always a very handsome briefcase. Black, good leather—you know? Usually it was facedown, but one morning I saw initials on it in gold. But they weren't hers. I knew her name by then."

"Do you remember what they were?"

"There could've been an M, but I wouldn't swear to it."

Mitchell, I thought. Maybe they used Mitchell in the building where they lived and also where they worked, but not in any of the places they frequented nearby. Then no one they ran into could connect them to their apartment, send them a letter, or find them if they were being sought by someone potentially dangerous. I thought again that there must be a PO box somewhere where they picked up their mail, or perhaps they rented a box at one of those private places that have sprung up in the last ten years.

"Good tea," I said.

"My daughter brought it from London for me. You ever been to London?"

"I've been out of the country only once and I was nowhere near London, but it's on my long-term list."

"You'll love it when you get there. I used to go with my husband when we were both healthy. That's a long time ago now." She looked sad for a moment. "You have children?"

"A little boy in kindergarten."

"Aren't you lucky." She smiled. "Anything else, dear? It was so nice of you to take me home. I hope you'll call and tell me about Rosette when you know something."

"I will."

She wrote down her phone number and address in my notebook. "There. Don't forget now."

"You'll hear from me." I gave her my phone number in case she remembered anything else, but I assured her she had been more helpful than anyone else I'd talked to. "The Bs in the license plate will probably give us the name of the owner of the vehicle."

"Big car," Gladys said. "Dark red. Hate 'em but everybody needs one these days. You know what?"

"What?"

"The last time I saw Rosette, she didn't have any polish on her nails. She must have been getting ready for a new manicure."

"I see." That meant Gladys had seen Rosette close to the end of her life.

We shook hands and she walked to the front door with me, then stood at the living room window so she could wave as I backed out of the driveway and turned down the block.

6

"We should be able to find the registration with that," Jack said. "Can't be more than a thousand, can there? And they won't all be SUVs."

"I haven't called Joe about it. Do you think I should?" I knew the answer to that. What I wanted was for Jack to find the registration, but I knew what my duty was. I had to turn my information over to the county police.

"You want a short answer or a long answer?"

"OK. I'll do what's right. But then I think I should give this investigation up. If I have to give Joe Fox everything I dig up, I may as well let his people dig it up for themselves."

"If they can."

"Well, Gladys French was a stroke of luck. There was nothing clever or original about my finding her. In a way she found me. She heard me talking to someone in the drugstore. And she recognized the picture."

"However it happened, you came up with the best information they've gotten. I'm sure they'll find the registration and the whole plate number from those Bs."

"I'll call Joe in the morning."

* * *

"Now, how did you come up with that?" the good detective said when I gave him the Bs.

I told him briefly, along with the fact that the victim gave her name to Gladys French as Rosette Parker.

"Well, I'll recommend you for a gold shield for that, Mrs. Brooks." The gold shield is a detective's badge. You can't apply for it; you can't take a test for it. They give it to you because you have earned it.

"I appreciate that, Joe. I'll wear it around my neck when I go to complain about my phone bill."

He laughed at that. "What's next on your agenda?"

"I think it's time for me to give up. You're the professionals. Whatever I dig up, you can do yourselves, and I don't want to get in your way. If I hear anything, which I don't expect to, I'll give you a call."

"Likewise. By the way, we have results on the prints we lifted in the apartment. No police record on any prints."

"I didn't think this was done by a career criminal," I said. "The killer had some kind of grudge or the Mitchells betrayed a trust. Maybe one stole from the other a long time ago, or some terrible accident occurred and the victim's family never accepted it was an accident."

"Those are good theories, Mrs. Brooks. Keep working on them."

We chatted a bit more and then finished our conversation. I must admit I was at loose ends after I hung up. I had gotten myself into the spirit of the chase, and having bowed out, I felt let down. There were things I could do, of course. I volunteer my time at the local parish to do whatever is necessary, including cleaning up the classrooms, not a very appealing alternative to hunting down a killer. It was a while since I had done word processing for my friend Arnold Gold, the lawyer. It was also some time since we'd met in the city for lunch, and I had an open invitation that I could accept at any time he wasn't in court or otherwise busy working for his clients. That was tempting. I looked at my calendar, which was largely empty, and was about to call Arnold when the phone rang.

"Chris, I've got something for you," my husband said.

"What? Have you talked to Joe?"

"Not yet. I decided to run that partial plate number. Did you give it to him?"

"About half an hour ago."

"Then I'm not stepping on toes. There's a maroon van-type vehicle registered to a Charles Proctor with a box number address—at least it looks like one of those mailboxes at a private company. It's the only maroon van with three Bs in the plate number in that zip code."

"Charles Proctor," I said. "Boy, they really have a lot of names."

"I also looked for a driver's license under both of his names and both of hers. Did you say she drove?"

"Yes. She was always driving when she picked up Gladys French. The husband sat in the backseat and read the paper."

"Well, there's no license for her under Mitchell or Parker, but there's one for him under Proctor. So he registered the car and got his license under the same name as is on the mailbox. Maybe he did his taxes under that name, too."

"Did you check for a driver's license for a woman at that mailbox address?"

"I did and there isn't any. Maybe she has her own box somewhere else."

"I'd go nuts with all those identities," I said.

"So would I. I think you're right about them. They were

hiding from someone and doing a damn good job of it. Finding Gladys French was fantastic luck."

"Well, I told Joe I'm resigning from the case. He'll find out what you just told me as soon as he runs the plate number, and he'll have to take it from there. In all the other cases I've looked into, I wasn't working parallel with the police. Sooner or later I'll get underfoot and there'll be a lot of resentment."

"They'll miss you when you're gone, honey."

I smiled. "You bet they will. I'm just going to sit back and wait for them to come begging." I told him Joe promised me a gold shield.

That brought a laugh. "I worked my butt off for my gold shield. Joe must be turning to mush."

Mush or not, I decided not to go to the place where the Proctor mailbox was. Instead, I wrote down the names I had for the husband and those for the wife and indicated under each one where it was used.

Mitchell was the at-home name for both of them and so far used nowhere else, unless the M Gladys had spotted on the briefcase meant that Mrs. Mitchell used that name at work. Rosette Parker was the name she used away from home—with the manicurist and Gladys French. I had no Parker name for the husband. But he used Charles Proctor for his license and registration. Was it possible the wife used Proctor for her license, too?

If there was a pattern, it needed to be filled in. I wondered whether the wife had her own mailbox, perhaps somewhere other than where her husband's was. *What were these people hiding from?*

Eddie came home and we had lunch together. He asked to visit a friend who had a backyard swimming pool. I am very nervous about children and backyard pools, but I knew the mother and trusted her. The pool was enclosed by a high metal fence that was gated and locked. I made the phone call and agreed to drive Eddie over at two. We went upstairs and found the one pair of bathing trunks that still fit.

"We'll have to buy you some more if you're going to swim a lot this summer."

"I want to swim. We can go to the Oakwood pool, can't we?"

"Sure. I joined last week."

"That's a much bigger pool than Terry's."

"It's for a lot of people. The whole town swims there."

"Then why does Terry have his own pool?"

"I guess his parents like having it."

"Can we get a pool in our backyard? We have a big backyard."

"No, Eddie, we can't. I enjoy swimming in a big pool so I can take lots of strokes before I have to turn around."

That gave him something to think about. I drove him over to Terry's, talked to Terry's mother for a while, then returned home. I was seriously thinking of putting on my own bathing suit and taking a quick swim in the town pool when the phone rang.

"Mrs. Brooks, it's Detective Palermo."

"Yes, hello."

"I just gave Detective Fox a call and thought I'd update you, too. There's been a development."

"In the Mitchell murder?"

He laughed. "You've asked me a question I can't answer. I don't know if it's related to the Mitchell murder. It's just a development till we get some more information. Another body has turned up."

"Really!"

"This time it's a man. Probably died around the time the woman did. There's a lot of decomposition, as you'd expect, but there's evidence of a gunshot wound."

"A gunshot wound." I was astounded. "Where was the body found?"

"Not in Oakwood, so it's not in our jurisdiction. It was also along the creek, but farther west, in the next town. They called me because they knew we'd found the woman's body and thought there might be a connection."

As did I. "How soon will you have a sketch?"

"Not today. That's for sure. I think Detective Fox will have to take care of that. I take it you'd like to see it?"

"I'd like to show it to someone."

"I'll ask Detective Fox to see to it that you get a copy."

"Thank you very much. And Detective Palermo? I really appreciate your calling to tell me."

"Well, you started things off. Have a nice day."

As incongruous as his sign-off was, I took it in the spirit in which I was sure it had been delivered. Then I sat down to think.

They had killed Peter Mitchell, too. It took a minute or so before I realized I had thought "they" not "he." There must be two of them, a man and a woman. The second, more distant voice on the phone had been a man's. Perhaps the phone call to me had, as Joe suggested, been some kind of setup.

I looked at my watch. I really did want to swim. It was hot out today and I had my membership card. I didn't need to pick up Eddie for a couple of hours and I hadn't been in the pool since the end of last summer. Suddenly, I could almost taste the water, sparkling blue where the afternoon sun hit it.

I pulled on one of last year's suits, looked at myself

with slight misgivings in the bathroom mirror, grabbed a cover-up and a towel, and drove off. The parking lot was only half full and I was able to park in relative shade. A new high school face greeted me at the entrance and OK'd my card.

A number of people from the area where we lived, from the church, and from the school waved and said hello as I passed. I stopped only briefly, the shimmering water as inviting as I had ever seen it. I picked a lounge, left my towel, bag, and sandals, and made my way to the water. It was quite cool, but this was early in the season. I went in by degrees, finally dipping my body up to my shoulders. And then I was off.

I am not a strong swimmer but I am an enthusiastic one. I had one of the reserved lap lanes to myself, and I glided back and forth, regaining my dormant skills. Finally, I let my mind travel back to thoughts of the Mitchells.

The essential question was still unanswered: What had the Mitchells done to enrage the man and woman, according to my logic, who had hunted them down and killed them? Maybe the Mitchells had bilked them out of money. Maybe the Mitchells were con artists who had gone too far with a mark.

I came to the end of the lane once again and decided I'd had enough for a first dip in the pool. As I usually did, I lay on my lounge under a huge shade tree and let myself dry. I had a book with me, but I was too consumed with the Mitchell homicides to concentrate on reading. One thing I knew for sure: This was not a crime of the moment. This crime had been planned for years and executed accordingly. What puzzled me was how I fit into it. The woman had known my full name and who I was in the community. I believed I had been talking to a killer, not a victim. She must have known that by alerting me I would stir the pot, so why did she call me that day in May?

"They're all interesting questions," Jack said in the evening. "And I can't answer them any more than you can. But I agree this wasn't a crime of opportunity. These people were marked for death, hunted for the kill. By the way, we don't yet know that the dead man is the husband of Holly Mitchell."

"True, but it's a good bet."

"Joe promised to fax me the sketches as soon as they're drawn. The autopsy is scheduled for tomorrow."

"I hope the artist has enough to work with."

"They have special guys that do that sort of thing. Remember when you got someone to make a head sculpture for you a few years ago and then he changed the age?"

I did remember. It had been fascinating to see. "OK. I'll just wait for the sketch. I want to show it to Gladys."

"I'm sure the cops'll show it to the building manager and the neighbors. Someone there'll ID him."

"What I need is someone from the past, one person who can place that couple in a city where they were known before they started running. It's as though they built a concrete wall around themselves and someone has to crack it open. If we could get those sketches on TV, maybe someone would come forward."

"You're not getting it on national TV," my husband the realist said. "And if they come from the Midwest or the West, no one in New York City is likely to have known them."

I found out the next day that the driver's license for Charles Proctor had a photo on it. That would give something to compare a sketch to, when it was done. The medical examiner was able to lift fingerprints from the body in spite of the decomposition. What they did, Jack told me, was inflate the fingers with a gas, press the fingertips on an inked board as though they were living fingers, and then roll them on special paper. In this case, as in the case of Holly, the prints were clear enough to be usable.

The man's death had indeed been caused by a gunshot, one to be exact. The shooter had stood in front of him and aimed at his heart. The bullet was found inside him, a .38 caliber lead slug fired from close range, leaving tattooing on the clothes and some on the skin. The bullet had carried cloth threads into the entry wound. The lab report stated that the muzzle of the gun was approximately two inches away when the weapon was fired.

Joe Fox assured me there would have been plenty of blood. The ME's office would analyze the blood in the body for DNA and compare it to the stains found in the apartment bedroom. Perhaps now there would be a match.

The man had been wearing a business suit but there was no wallet or other means of identification on him. An indentation on his left ring finger indicated he had worn a wedding ring for a long time. His shirt was a common brand available in many stores, and the suit, while moderately expensive, could be bought in any number of outlets. Neither victim had worn shoes and none of their clothing had a store label.

The man, however, had a scar from an appendectomy done many years ago. I didn't think that would be of much help, though, as appendectomies are common.

The police still didn't know what had killed the woman.

Joe Fox said that an enlarged version of the license photo had been recognized by the building manager, but not with great certainty. It was the wife who usually came down if there was a problem, and there weren't many problems with the Mitchells. But the woman across the hall, the one who had said she didn't have much to do with them, recognized both the picture of the man and the sketch of the woman. A few other tenants thought the couple looked vaguely familiar.

But the man who had seen people loading the vehicle with furniture said he just couldn't be sure about the man.

7

In the morning, Jack called with a ballistics report from Joe Fox. "The bullet was nice and clean," Jack said. "The ballistics guy said it had nice lands and grooves. It was either a new gun or a new barrel."

The lands and grooves, as Jack had explained to me in the past, referred to the markings on the lead bullet. The tiny markings are the result of the lead bullet passing through the steel gun barrel and rubbing against the riflings inside. These riflings, which are spiraled grooves, cause a bullet to rotate around its longer axis prior to exiting the muzzle of the gun. Using a microscope, ballistics experts compare bullets and can tell when two or more have been fired from the same gun. As a barrel becomes old, much used, or pitted, the markings on the bullet change and blur. Changing the gun barrel changes the markings on the bullet.

Jack had also received by fax sketches of the second victim, which he would take home with him tonight. "Maybe we need a fax at home," he said. Now that we had a computer, he seemed interested in adding appendages to it, and I, the nervous money manager of the family, kept telling him all these things he considered both wonderful and necessary would get little if any use. When I left St.

Stephen's and took up a secular life, I bounced into the end of the twentieth century with a start. I was reluctant to move much further, especially when all these addenda were three figures apiece.

"Don't do anything precipitous," I cautioned, knowing it would have no effect. Jack's office at One PP is in that part of New York that is filled with enticing electronics outlets, and he is easily enticed.

"What's on your agenda today?"

"I want to talk to the building manager. I know the police have questioned him, but I'd like to do it myself."

"Aren't you the gal who said she was keeping out of this case?"

"You know me, Jack. No self-restraint."

"Well, I think the building manager's a good idea. You may pick up something they overlooked. See you later."

I drove over to the apartments and found him just walking into his office. "Mr. Stone, I'm Chris Bennett Brooks. We met last month when I came over with Detective Palermo."

A frown smoothed into a welcoming look. "Mrs. Brooks, yes, I remember. That was the day we found the apartment empty."

"Right."

"Sit down. What can I do for you?"

"I suppose you heard that Mrs. Mitchell's body was found last week."

"Yeah. And his body turned up a coupla days ago."

"Right."

"Have they figured out for sure if it's Mr. Mitchell's yet?"

"I don't know. I'm kind of assuming it is."

"Stands to reason."

"I'm interested in this case because I got that phone call last month, the day I came over with Detective Palermo."

"Sure."

"The case has been moved to the sheriff's division."

"I know. And they're a pain in the rear, if you know what I mean."

"How so?"

"They've questioned me about a hundred times. I keep telling them I don't know anything and then they come back again and ask the same things. It's like they think I'm keeping something to myself and I'm not."

"I'm sorry to hear it," I said, thinking that could be quite an annoyance. "I wonder if you'd mind talking to me about the Mitchells. I promise I won't bother you."

He gave me a grin. "That's OK. I wasn't complaining about you. But I don't know what I can tell you. They kept to themselves and I didn't see them much. They were generous at Christmas, I'll tell you that."

That didn't surprise me. They wanted to keep on good terms with this man. If anyone ever came asking questions, he might not answer them if he thought it would jeopardize his end-of-the-year gift. "Did anyone ever ask about them? When they were alive, I mean?"

"Not that I recall. They must have paid their bills on time. They didn't have a beef with anyone that I know of."

"Did anyone ever come looking for them?"

"Never."

"Were packages for them left with you?"

He thought a minute. "Maybe once in a while. Yeah. I think so."

"Do you remember where those packages came from?"

"Uh, no. One was UPS—I'm sure of that."

"How long ago?"

"Coupla months."

"Any sent by mail?" I was desperate for a return address.

"Could've been. I just don't remember. I get a lot of packages here. I just wait for folks to come around and pick them up. I don't really look at the packages."

"Do you know if they had visitors? Either overnight or just for the evening?"

"I can't even see their entrance from here. I wouldn't know. That woman who lives across the way would be your best bet."

"How long did they live here, by the way?"

"Almost two years. There's only a couple of months or so left on their lease."

"Do you know where they came from?" I knew the building management company would have ordered a financial report on the Mitchells and that the police would have already gotten their rental file.

He got up and went to the file cabinet in the corner of the office. "Out of state," he said, reading from a file folder. "They didn't have any local references, but they gave us three months' rent in advance so we gave them the apartment. They never paid late and they always paid in cash—you wouldn't believe how many checks bounce in this place, and these people are supposed to be so rich—so I'd say they were good tenants. We didn't make a mistake."

"Do you know if they had children?"

"They could've, but I never saw any around here, not young ones, anyway. If anyone was living with them in that apartment, I don't know about it."

"Mr. Stone, I'm going to leave you my name and phone number. If you remember anything or if someone should happen to come in asking for the Mitchells, I'd appreciate a call."

"Sure thing. You're a lot easier to talk to than that cop. He really makes me nervous."

"Well, I'm glad I didn't." I wrote down my usual information and gave it to him. He studied it for a moment, then stuck it in the edge of the blotter on his desk. We shook hands and I left. I hadn't learned much, but I thought I'd made a better impression than the person who'd been hounding him.

In the evening, Jack came home with the sketches. They were a good match with the driver's license photo so we assumed that the body was that of Peter Mitchell and Charles Proctor. The next morning, Friday, I called Gladys French and asked if I could come over. She was thrilled to hear from me, delighted I wanted to visit. Although she invited me for lunch, I declined.

She nearly kissed me as I entered her house an hour later. "How nice to see you again," she said with a big smile. "Come in and make yourself at home."

I did just that, sitting on a worn but comfortable chair in her living room. I handed her the sketch and the license photo.

She nodded. "That's him."

"Who?" I asked, wanting a positive identification.

"Rosette's husband. That's the man who sat in the back of their car and read the *Times* every day."

"I think I told you they may have used more than one name. You're sure you never heard her call him by name?"

"The first time she picked me up, she said something like, 'That's my husband in the backseat with his nose in the paper.' I just thought of him as Mr. Parker."

"OK."

"That's it? That's all you wanted to ask? I thought you were going to tell me you found the person who killed Rosette."

"We haven't. And the reason I'm asking you about the man in this picture is that his body was found the day after I talked to you."

"What?"

"I'm afraid so."

"Oh my God. Who would do such a thing, Christine? Who could be so cruel as to kill such a nice couple?"

"I have no idea. But we're sure now that this is Rosette's husband, and we know someone killed both of them."

"Terrible," Gladys said, shaking her head and looking gloomy. "What's happening in this world?"

It wasn't a question I could answer and I didn't try to. I stayed a few minutes longer, asked if I could drive her anywhere, and left when she said she had no errands that day, that she intended to do a little weeding in the back. It was good exercise and the garden needed it.

I knew I didn't have to ask Larry Stone to ID the sketch. The detestable cop would have been at his doorstep the minute the sketch was completed. What I did was drive out of Oakwood and go to a few banks with my pictures to see if the couple, by any name, had had an account.

I tried a number of banks with no success. I began to think they might maintain an account far from New York State, perhaps where they had once lived or even a place where they had never lived. The police might be able to locate such an account if they had the correct Social Security number, but as far as I knew, no such number was known at the moment. And I didn't have the access that the police did.

It was disheartening, but not unexpected. I was starting

to get hungry when I saw a small bank down the street from where I had parked my car. There was just enough time to drop in and give it a try.

The bank was almost empty, only one young mother with two preschool children standing at a window. I found a single desk occupied and sat down in the chair beside it. The woman identified as manager smiled and asked what she could do for me.

"I wonder if either of these people might be customers of the bank," I said, laying the sketches on the desk.

"He doesn't look familiar. May I ask what this is about?"

"These people were Oakwood residents who have apparently been murdered."

"Are they the ones whose bodies—?" She seemed incapable of articulating the facts.

"That's right. No one knows who exactly they are and where they come from. I knew them slightly and I have some time, so I thought I'd do some digging. I don't suppose the police have been here?"

"Not that I'm aware of. Let me see the woman." She picked the sketch up and inspected it. "She came in here and opened an account but it was a long time ago. I didn't see her in the bank again so I assume she used the drive-up or the ATM. And I can't remember her name."

"Would you recognize it?"

"I can look it up."

"Holly Mitchell."

She turned to her computer and keyed in the name. I couldn't see the screen but I watched her face. She shook her head. "I don't get a hit on that name."

"Rosette Parker."

She typed again. "She's a customer, yes. But I can't swear she's that woman in the picture."

"That's good enough. Can you tell me if you sent her statements to this address?" I wrote down the apartment address.

She checked her screen. "No, they went to a box number. It's kind of coming back to me now. She said she'd had a lot of trouble with mail delivery and she didn't want important things going to where she lived. I can't disclose the box number, but I can tell you where the box is."

"Thank you."

She wrote it down and handed me the paper. It was one of those Mail Boxes places.

"Is the account in her name alone?" I asked.

"Yes, Rosette Parker. There's no one else."

"I assume it's a checking account."

"That's right. It's the only account she has with us."

I gave her the two names I had for the husband and she checked both of them with no luck. It appeared that Rosette wrote the checks for the family or her husband banked elsewhere.

"When did she open the account?" I asked.

"About two years ago. This is amazing. What a terrible thing to happen."

"Do you have a Social Security number for this woman?"

"Yes, indeed. We can't open an account without one. But I can't disclose it."

"I understand. Thank you very much for your time, Mrs. Hanover," I said, reading her name off her desk sign.

I went home and had lunch. Eddie was with a friend today and I didn't have to pick him up till late afternoon. When I had finished the last of my tomato juice and sandwich, I called Joe Fox.

"That sounds like a good day's work," he said. "How did you find the bank?"

"I drove out of Oakwood toward White Plains, just on the chance that they might use a bank on the way to work. This is quite a small one, just a storefront. I'm surprised it hasn't been grabbed by one of those invaders that are scooping up banks all over the place."

"That's probably why we missed it," Joe said, but I thought I heard a sigh. "We've been looking into the conglomerates without any luck at all."

"You can talk to Mrs. Hanover. She's the manager. She seemed to recognize the sketches and Rosette Parker came up on her computer. She has a Social Security number for Rosette but she wouldn't give it to me, of course."

"Of course. And it may be a made-up one. But thanks for the hard work, Mrs. Brooks. Looks like you're not resigning the case after all."

"It's in my blood, Joe. What can I do?"

What can I do? was the operative phrase I hear them say all the time on TV. I had the bank and I had the location of their mailbox, both of which Joe's men would check out. And now I couldn't think for the life of me what to do next. With Social Security numbers the police might be able to trace the Mitchells' previous residence, but I suspected they changed numbers as regularly as they changed addresses. I had never encountered a case with so many dead ends. It was a lesson for me. Change your names and numbers and move frequently, and you're very hard to find. Except a killer had managed to do it.

8

It was an enjoyable weekend. I worked in the garden, took Eddie to the town pool, and watched him regain the skills of last year. He was as enthusiastic a swimmer as his parents, which delighted me. There was no news from any source about the Mitchells, and I had begun to wonder whether their pasts had been so well hidden that they would never be uncovered.

On Saturday, while Jack and Eddie were spending time together, I took myself to the place along the creek where Peter Mitchell's body had been found. It was farther down the creek than the woman's and better hidden, just over the town line. His killer had dug a shallow grave, while she had just been pushed under shrubs and then covered with branches, leaves, and other vegetation. The man's body was discovered after a rain, when his foot, clad in a black sock, began to protrude from the damp earth. A dog, who had stopped and sniffed, motivated its owner to have a look.

By the time I arrived on the scene, four days after the discovery, the crime scene tape and uniformed police were gone. But it had become a tourist site, with a few visitors leaving small bouquets. I listened to the conversation of the people standing around, but it was clear they knew a lot less about the case than I did.

The autopsies could not determine the exact time of the deaths of the two victims, and the medical examiner did not know which person had been murdered first or buried first. The best he could do was approximate, and the time spans he gave were the same.

On Monday, when I was straightening up after a hectic Sunday that had seen my cousin Gene and Eddie running around with abandon, the phone rang.

"Mrs. Brooks?" A man.

"Yes."

"Hi, this is Larry Stone, the building manager, remember?"

"Larry, yes. Good morning. What's up?"

"I've got someone here I think you should talk to."

"Oh?"

"Yeah. She hasn't given me a name but she doesn't want to talk to the police and I don't blame her. I told her about you and maybe she'll talk to you. You want to drive over and pick her up?"

"She doesn't have a car?"

"She came by taxi."

"I'll be there in ten minutes."

I had no idea what to expect but it sounded as though the woman might be from out of town. Either that or she was elderly. Anyone else around here would have a car.

I parked near Larry Stone's office and walked around to his entrance. The door was half open, a doorstop in place. It was going to be a warm day but still possible to get fresh air in the morning as long as the door or window didn't face due east.

"Mrs. Brooks, hi."

"Hi, Larry." He had stood from his desk chair. I looked to the left and saw a slim, fragile-looking girl with dark hair pulled back sitting in a wooden chair near the filing cabinet. She looked at me with curious eyes, but said nothing.

"That's her. She won't give me a name. She's all yours."

I estimated her age as early twenties. "I'm Chris Bennett Brooks," I said. "You're here about Mr. and Mrs. Mitchell?"

"I'm looking for them. I went to the apartment last night and no one answered. I waited until midnight and they didn't come home."

I turned to Larry. "What have you told her?"

"Nothin'. I'm not getting involved."

"Are you their daughter?" I asked.

"Yes."

"Why don't you come with me? I'll tell you all about it. Do you have any luggage?"

"It's at the motel."

I said, "Thanks, Larry," and led the unnamed young woman to my car.

"Where are we going?" she asked in a nervous voice. "I want to stay here and wait for them."

"They're not coming back here. We'll go to my house and I'll explain everything."

"They moved again."

"That's part of it."

"I went inside the apartment last night and again this morning. It's empty. I can't understand why they didn't tell me where they were going."

I didn't want to tell her in the car, partly because I could not foresee her reaction and partly because I hadn't prepared myself for this. I was about to inform a young woman that both of her parents were not only dead, but murdered. It was a burden I did not want, but I thought it might be better coming from me than from Larry Stone or the cop he couldn't stand.

We drove in silence to my house. I left the car in the drive and took her inside. "Would you like something cool to drink?" I asked.

"Water?" she said.

"Sure. Or you could have homemade lemonade." Mel had given me a recipe and we all loved it.

"That would be nice." She smiled, and I thought I saw a resemblance between her face and the sketch of Holly Mitchell.

I poured two glasses and led her to the family room. When she was sitting with her lemonade on the table beside her, I said, "Your parents aren't coming back to Oakwood."

"Something's happened."

"Something terrible. I'm sorry to be the one to tell you. Your—"

"They've been murdered, haven't they?"

And suddenly I was the one who was shocked. "Yes. How did you know that?"

Her lips trembled and she pressed them together. Her eyes were full. "It's what they feared," she said in a whisper.

"Someone was after them?"

She nodded, unable to speak. She put her hands up to her face and breathed through sobs. "Yes," she was finally able to say. "Yes. Someone was after them. I don't know who, but they did."

"Miss Mitchell—"

"Ariana. My name's Ariana."

"Ariana, you don't have to talk about it now. I know this is a terrible shock. But when you're ready, we should talk. The police are investigating the case. I'm an amateur with some experience and I'm looking into it because of a phone call I got telling me there was going to be a body found. I don't know who it came from or why the woman called me, but I got the police over there and we found the empty apartment."

"I'd like to wash my face, please."

I took her to the downstairs bathroom, grateful that I kept a guest towel on an extra rack. I wasn't sure how to proceed. The proper action would be to call Joe Fox and have him take over, but Larry Stone had said she didn't want the police called. I felt uneasy keeping her existence a secret, but I didn't want to betray her. While I waited, I refilled the lemonade glasses.

She was gone almost ten minutes and when she returned, her face looked damp. "Thank you," she said. "I think I can talk now. I don't want anything to do with the police. If you promise me you won't call them, I'll tell you what I know—and what I don't know."

"For now I won't call them. And the building manager over at the apartments won't call them either. One of the cops was annoying him, which is why he called me this morning."

"First tell me what you know of my parents' deaths."

I went through it from the moment I picked up the telephone that afternoon in May. I had taken the trouble to write down what I recalled of the conversation so that I would get it right if I was questioned again by another branch of law enforcement. Jack had intimated that the FBI might be called in at some point, but that had not happened. I brought my notebook into the family room and read to her the conversation as I had recorded it.

She watched me with a face that looked mystified and horrified. "This woman called and said a murder was going to take place?" she asked.

"Not exactly. I wasn't even sure whether it had taken place or it was going to. Then I heard the explosion and then the phone was hung up."

"And that's when you called the police."

"That's when I went to the police station to try to get someone to figure out who had called me and from where."

"I see."

When I reached the point of the discovery of Holly Mitchell's body, she began to cry again. I asked her if she wanted to see the sketch and she nodded. She held it with trembling fingers, tears running down her face. "That's my mother," she whispered. She ran her fingers over the hardened drops of pink nail polish and I explained where that came from.

"She always had her nails done," Ariana said. "She said they made a lady of a woman." She looked down at her own well-shaped nails, glossy with colorless polish. Ariana was also a lady.

I handed her the sketch of the man. I could feel her agony.

"Where are they?" she asked.

"In the morgue, but I don't know the location. I can find out."

"I don't want to see them in that condition. I want to remember them alive. I want to remember them as the active, loving people they were."

"I understand."

I continued my narrative, telling her everything I had learned on my own and everything Joe Fox had told me. She asked almost no questions, content to listen intently. Suddenly I said, "Have you had breakfast?"

"No. But the lemonade is fine."

"Let me give you something more substantial. Juice? English muffin? Coffee?"

"No coffee, thanks. But the rest would be fine."

I prepared it quickly and gave it to her, setting it on a tray table I kept in a closet. I sat quietly while she spread butter and jam on the toasted muffin.

"The juice is good."

"It's real. It's one of our small pleasures."

She smiled at that. When she had finished eating, she said, "So you don't know how my mother died."

"Not yet. I'll get a report from the detective in charge as soon as he knows. Things move somewhat slowly here. This isn't New York with its high-tech equipment and many experienced medical examiners."

"And Dad had a bullet in him?"

"Yes."

"So that could have been the sound you heard on the phone."

"It could have, but more and more I think that's not what happened. I think they were both dead when the phone call was made. I think the phone call was to alert me—and through me the police—that a homicide had taken place; a double homicide, as it turned out. We'll never know exactly when they were murdered unless we catch the killers and they tell us the truth. But I suspect the bodies had been hidden before I got the call, and as soon as the call ended, the killer or killers took off. I have no idea where they could be now."

"I don't either. But it's possible my parents knew they were close, which is why they had moved their possessions out of the apartment."

"It's possible. I think that might have happened."

"They always seemed to sense when they got close."

"Then this happened before?"

"Many times. Well, several times. But they always let me know when and where they were going. I might have been able to help them." Her eyes teared up. "Now it's too late."

"Who were they running from, Ariana?"

She shrugged. "I wish I knew."

"Did they know? I mean, did they know the name of the person who was after them?"

"I think so. But they kept it to themselves. They didn't want to worry me any more than they had to."

"Do you know where your parents worked?"

"My mother worked in White Plains for a small public relations company. She had a lot of experience in that. She had done it in other cities. Dad changed jobs recently and I'm not sure where he worked."

"Do you know the name of the firm your mother worked for?"

She picked her large bag up off the floor. It was one of those Italian straw slings that can be stuffed and overstuffed, although finding something often meant digging. I watched her dig. Finally, she pulled out a small black book and leafed through the pages. "I have the address and phone number here," she said. "I wrote it in my calendar on the date of Mom's birthday. That way I didn't have to put it under her name."

"You live a careful life."

"They trained me to be careful. Here."

I reached for the book and wrote down the information in my notebook. "Did you ever call her there?" I asked.

"Yes. I probably talked to her a day or so before they . . . disappeared. I remember now that Mom sounded a little funny, as though she might be keeping something from me. She said we'd talk again in a couple of days and I shouldn't call her at work again. So I didn't. I called the number at the apartment. They didn't have an answering machine because they didn't want people to leave messages. I let it ring and ring but no one answered. It wasn't the first time this had happened so I assumed I'd hear from them eventually. But I didn't. I thought about it and worried and finally I called the office in White Plains. I got my mother's voice mail but that didn't tell me anything. It was the usual. 'I'm away from my desk, da-dah, da-dah.' I didn't leave a message. Finally, at the end of last week, I called again and someone else answered. That scared me. I realized she might not be there anymore. No one was answering at the apartment, so I came here and went to the apartment."

"And found it empty."

"Yes." It was almost a whisper.

I was about to ask her something when the phone rang. "Excuse me," I said and jumped up. It was Jack.

"I heard from Joe Fox. He tells me they're—"

"Quickly," I said in a low voice. "I'm interviewing someone."

"In the house?"

"It's OK. Go on."

"Watch it, Chris. You never know—"

"I know."

"Joe says they got back some of the toxicology results

and the cause of death of the woman is still a mystery. They're bringing someone else in to do a second autopsy."

"That's surprising. When will it take place?" I glanced toward the family room where Ariana sat almost unmoving.

"Today, I think. Maybe we'll know something tonight. I thought some kind of poison might show up but it hasn't."

"Thanks, honey," I said.

"Can you tell me who you're talking to?"

"A kid," I said, hoping the syllable would not carry.

"A child of the Mitchells?"

"Yes."

"Who turned up this morning?"

"Yes."

"You call Joe?"

"Absolutely not."

There was one of those silences that let me know he disagreed with me. "You know how I feel about holding back information."

"I do. But for the moment I have no choice."

"Well, for the moment then, my lips are sealed."

I hoped the same thing would not be true of Joe Fox's.

9

"Sorry," I said, sitting down again.

"That's all right."

"Ariana, what I'd like to know from you is essentially a biography of your life: when you realized something was strange in your parents' lives, what they told you, every place you've lived in, where they worked, what you've done with yourself."

"And the reason you want to know all this is—?"

"Because somewhere in the past is an event or a group of events that made someone want to kill your parents."

"Yes." She didn't look at me. Perhaps she was considering the consequences of telling me the things I wanted to know. Perhaps it had occurred to her that her parents, these wonderful people whom she loved so much, had once done another person a terrible injustice. She might think that it was better to let the killer go free than to have to own up to her parents' indiscretions, to allow them to become public.

"If you're up to it."

"Chris, my parents were good people," she said, confirming my suspicion.

"I'm sure they were. You of all people would know. Do you have brothers or sisters?"

She shook her head. "My mother once said something about not being able to have more children."

"How old are you?"

"Twenty-three."

"Where do you work?"

"In Chicago. I went there after college and got a job in a bookstore."

"I bet that's fun."

"It is. It's a wonderful store, near the university. We get so many interesting people coming in." She spoke with an enthusiasm any employer would delight in.

"I've never been to Chicago," I said.

"It's a beautiful city. The lake is so lovely. You can drive along it to all the beautiful towns north of Chicago." She stopped. "You're not interested in all this. You want to find a killer. All right. I want to find him, too. I'll tell you everything I remember."

I flipped to a new page in my notebook. "Start as far back as you can recall."

She drank some lemonade and pressed the napkin delicately to her lips. She came across as a well-behaved young woman who had learned the niceties of life and practiced them easily. She was wearing a long beige skirt with the texture of chambray and a matching blouse of the same fabric that covered the waist. The two top buttons were open but she still retained a demure look. Her fingers were ringless but two silver bracelets encircled her right wrist while on her left was a watch that she glanced at frequently. A pair of thin gold hoop earrings adorned her earlobes. They were so fine, I hadn't noticed them till a few minutes ago.

"I was born in Portland, Oregon, but I don't remember it at all. My first clear memory is a house in San Diego, or maybe it was outside of San Diego. I was very young. I went to nursery school where I met a little Japanese girl and we were friends. I didn't know she was Japanese till someone told me. And the next thing I remember, we were living in Phoenix, Arizona."

"How old were you then?"

She thought. "Four. About that."

"House or apartment?"

"An apartment. It was very nice, sunny. My mother didn't work at first. She stayed home. Maybe she started to work when I went into kindergarten. I'm not sure."

"Do you remember an address?"

She thought. "A street. I think it was Cactus Lane. And the number was one-twenty." She seemed pleased to have remembered. "We lived in Two C. There was a little balcony we could sit on in the evening. It was so nice there."

"Friends? Any names at all?"

She shook her head. "My teacher was Miss Rodriguez—I'm sure of that."

That would have been sixteen or seventeen years ago. The teacher might still be around, but what would I learn from her? "And then?" I asked.

"I'm trying to remember where we went after that. Maybe that's when we moved to Wisconsin."

"That's some weather difference."

"I must have heard my mother complain about that a million times. She hated the summer in Phoenix, but she hated the winter in Wisconsin even more."

"Where did you live there?"

"In a house. I had a lovely little room, all decorated for me."

I let her ramble on, describing the room just made for a little girl. She had an excellent memory for details—what the curtains looked like, what toys were spread across the pillows. She had a favorite doll, a favorite bedtime story, a favorite television program. She went to school and found a best friend, a teacher she loved, a group of acquaintances. It sounded like a happy time in her life.

"I don't suppose you know whether your parents owned that house or rented."

"I have no idea. It was our house, that's all I know."

"You haven't mentioned grandparents or cousins or aunts and uncles. Did you have any?"

"I don't think so. Wait. There was a voice on the telephone. That was Grandma."

"Didn't she come to visit?"

"I don't remember ever seeing her."

"Do you know whose mother she was?"

"No idea. She was just Grandma, no last name."

"What about the family next door in Wisconsin?"

"Mrs. Palmer," she said quickly. "Old and gray and lived alone. People came to visit her on weekends sometimes. I don't know where they came from but they drove a long white station wagon. I never visited when she had company."

I asked her for the address, which she knew, and whether she could remember what work her parents did. Her father worked in an office. Her mother worked at the university, but Ariana wasn't sure at what.

That location lasted a few years. It was her feeling that the cold winters just got to be too much for her mother and they decided to move somewhere warmer. I could see how you could deceive a child into believing such a ruse. What does a child know about parents' real worries and real intentions? If I told Eddie we were moving to a bigger house because this one was too small for us, he would believe me.

"So you moved to a warmer clime," I said.

"Baltimore. We had a house there and we visited Washington, D.C., a lot. My mother loved the cherry blossoms and we went every year when they were in bloom. They were so beautiful." She smiled and stopped speaking, perhaps seeing the trees around the Tidal Basin. Then she said, "I went to a Catholic school there."

"Are you Catholic?"

"No, but my parents thought they had good schools and it was a good place for a girl to go."

"I taught in one," I said, "a women's college up the Hudson. How old were you by then?"

"About ten, I would think. Do you want the name and address of the school?"

"Yes, please." While I might not have special access to a Catholic school, my friend Sister Joseph, the general superior of St. Stephen's Convent, would surely be able to get information for me if I needed it. And since Ariana went to Catholic school only about a dozen years ago, there was a good chance there were still teachers there who would remember Ariana and her parents.

She wrote down the home address, the school address, and the names of some teachers she remembered. Then she went on, telling me where her parents had worked during the years they lived in Baltimore.

After Baltimore they did a stint in Boston, a city Ariana liked. She went to a Catholic high school there and then went to college in Pennsylvania. Her parents had crossed the country as she grew up and didn't want her too far from home, not more than half a day's drive, her mother said. That was all right with Ariana. She had Philadelphia down the road and friends from around the country.

"What made you decide to work in Chicago?" I asked.

"By that time I knew that my parents were running from someone. I had been in one place for four years and they wanted me to pick up and go somewhere else, make a new start. My father said it would make him sleep easier."

"So you've been in Chicago about as long as your parents were in Oakwood."

"Yes, just about."

"Now I want to ask you about the names you've used," I said.

She smiled a bit. "I knew this was coming."

"I've learned that your parents used the names Peter and Holly Mitchell in the apartment. Your mother was Rosette Parker at the bank and the place where she had her nails done. Your father was Charles Proctor on his driver's license and the registration of his vehicle."

She looked troubled. "How did you find all these things out? My parents were so careful."

"Part of it is that we knew they must be using other names because there was no car registered to Mitchell and we knew they drove one. My first break was the nail place. Your mother was identified there as Rosette Parker. I simply took it from there. A good part of it was luck," I conceded. "An old woman in the pharmacy recognized the sketch of your mother and said her license plate started with BBB. With that kind of information, together with the type of vehicle, the police were able to find the registration."

"That's scary."

"When did you become aware that your parents' lives were not the norm?"

"In my teens. Maybe when we moved to Boston, maybe before that. I asked my mother one day because by then I knew they used more than one name. At some point, before I went to college, I asked her what was going on."

"It must have been difficult for you," I said.

"It was terrible. A lot of things became clear—why I never met my grandmother, why I was never left with a babysitter, why mail went to a box, not to the house, a lot of things."

"And what did she tell you?"

"She said there had been a problem years ago and it was better if I didn't know what it was. That someone was very angry at them and had been looking for them for several years. I can't put a date on it, Chris. I don't know exactly when I asked the question and I have no idea when this incident happened. My parents were very careful about what they told me. Mom wouldn't answer my question till she and Dad had talked about it, and then the three of us sat down in the living room and discussed it. I was left feeling that I knew less when we finished than when we began. These were good, kind people who had spent their lives caring for me and loving me, and somehow they had enraged someone to the point that they had to run for their lives."

"Did you ever get a sense of what was behind it? Money? Real estate? A terrible and tragic accident?"

"I thought of all those things. I thought of worse things. They never gave me a clue."

"Do you know their real last name?" I asked.

"I know mine. I have my birth certificate. I'm Ariana Brinker. My mother is listed as Elaine and there's no maiden name. My father's first name was Ronald. Nobody called them by those names, except maybe where I went to school."

"So I guess the first time they moved, they changed names."

"Probably."

"Have you ever looked into their past? Tried to find relatives?"

"Never. They made it very clear that they feared for their lives. I've often wondered whether I had blood relatives out in Oregon but I couldn't put Mom and Dad in jeopardy. Or myself. What if this person wanted to kill me too?"

It was a possibility. "Ariana, the police want to find their killer or killers. Do you?"

"I haven't thought about it. I just found out this morning that they're dead. But yes, I want to know who did this and I want them punished."

"What if facts turn up that indicate your parents were involved in a terrible crime?"

She leaned back and looked away. Tears fell down her cheeks. I had posed an unanswerable question. If I were asked the same thing, I would know absolutely that my parents had never committed a crime. But her situation was different. She knew there was something unspeakable in their past.

"They never hurt anyone," she said finally, wiping the tears away with a tissue she took out of her bag. "If they stole money, it would have been to give me a safe, happy life, and I don't believe they stole. They both worked at good jobs and they were appreciated. Whenever they left, they were given parties and gifts. They were good people. You won't uncover the kind of crime I would be ashamed of hearing about."

"OK." I leaned back myself, letting her regain control.

"When you got that strange phone call, you don't know whether you were speaking to my mother or a possible killer."

"No idea. But there is one other thing. The woman said that day was her twenty-fifth wedding anniversary, her silver anniversary."

Ariana opened the little book in which she had found her mother's phone number at work and skimmed some pages. She read the date off to me.

"That sounds about right. It was a Tuesday, I remember."

"Yes, it was." She closed the book. "That was their twenty-fifth anniversary. You may have talked to my mother."

"Or someone who knew her well enough to know when her anniversary was."

"I don't know who that could be."

"I'm going to try to find out, Ariana."

"What about the police?"

"Let me say this. I won't tell them about you unless the building manager tells them something first. As far as we know, he's the only person around here who knows of your existence. But eventually I have to turn over what I find out."

"I understand." She dropped the little book in her bag. "I don't know why I trust you, but I guess I have to trust someone and you've been nice to me. All I ask is that you tell me what you know before you call the police."

"I will do that. Ariana, your parents were careful people. They must have told you what to do in case of their death."

"They did. I was just thinking about that. I know they

had a will written in Massachusetts when we lived there, but they did it again in New York State when they moved. I have a copy of their will but it's back home in Chicago. The lawyer's name and address are with the will. He may have instructions from them that I don't have."

"Have you read the will?"

"Just once when they gave me the copy. There's nothing complicated about it. I think they have bonds put away somewhere. It's all written down."

"Then I guess you'll have to go back and get it," I said.

"There's something else. I have to bury—" She stopped, overcome with grief. "My parents," she said finally.

"You'll have to identify yourself to claim them."

"I hate to think of them in a morgue. I want them safe in a nice green cemetery."

I said nothing. This was the big decision she had to make and she had to do it by herself.

"I tell you what," she said. "Let's give it two weeks. If we don't make any progress, I'll reconsider."

"That sounds reasonable."

"Now I think I should get back to the motel. I'm feeling tired and I need to rest and be alone."

"Do you have money?"

"That's not a problem."

"I'll drive you back."

10

Ariana Brinker was staying at the local motel where Sister Joseph had once stayed when we were working on a local homicide. I suggested she rest as long as she wanted and then call me. We could all have dinner together chez Brooks and plan a strategy later on in the evening. I told her I had a five-year-old and that we might be off at the town pool later in the afternoon, but she could leave a message.

Eddie and I left for the pool. His swimming was becoming more even and less like play and I was glad we had given him lessons last summer. He remembered how to coordinate his breathing, and I was pleased to see how much he wanted to continue learning. We swam side by side in a lap lane, and he was grinning when we came to the end.

Back home, we dressed and went downstairs to get dinner together. The phone rang as I was mixing good spices into our rosemary meat loaf. Might as well use the oven while the kitchen was still cool enough. We would have enough months of grilling starting anytime soon.

"This is Ariana."

"Did you sleep?"

"Yes. I didn't expect to. And I've made a reservation to

fly to Chicago tomorrow and return here on Wednesday. Is that all right with you?"

"It's fine. I assume you're going to pick up the will and come right back."

"Yes. And get some more clothes. I'll need to talk to the lawyer when I get back. I'm sure the name and address are with the will. I expect the lawyer has no idea my parents are dead."

"Right. You and I are the only two people at this point who know their real names."

I told her I would pick her up in twenty minutes. Then I let Eddie know we were having company for dinner. "Her name is Ariana," I said.

"Is she your friend?"

"She's a young lady I just met. She's very nice, honey. I think you'll like her. She works in a bookstore."

That provoked his interest. He started to tell me about all the books he needed.

"Maybe we'll go to our bookstore when school is out. You'll need some books to read over the summer." He wasn't exactly reading yet, but he knew what I meant.

I explained to Ariana that my husband was a police lieutenant in New York City. She tensed as I said it, but I assured her that since this case was out of his jurisdiction, he would not interfere. And he would be helpful if there was information we were not privy to as private citizens.

Ariana and Eddie seemed charmed by each other. I heard laughter from the family room as I set the table. Jack came home, having been forewarned by me. He shook hands with Ariana and expressed his condolences. She said a soft "Thank you" and brushed away welling tears.

When Eddie was tucked away, we sat in the family

room with coffee and a fruit pie I had picked up at the bakery after our swim. My Jewish friend Melanie told me that Jews offer sweets to the bereaved to ease their sorrow. That has stuck with me, sounding like a reasonable response to the anguish of loss.

"Jack," I said after we had chatted for a while, "Ariana and her parents lived in a number of locations around the country. And she was born in Portland, Oregon. We have some family names but no addresses. Is there a way we can find the phone numbers of these people on the Internet?"

"Boy," he said, "get them a computer and suddenly they're experts in tracking down missing people."

Ariana smiled. "Did you just get a computer?"

"At the end of last year," I said. "It had never occurred to me but Jack thought we should have one, especially since Eddie is starting to read and everyone he knows has one."

Jack said, "I'll check with a guy at work tomorrow—he's more computer literate than I am—and see how to proceed. It's a good idea. If you have your parents' names, you might find people with the same last name in Portland or nearby."

"And I remember people who lived near us in a couple of places. If they're still alive, we can talk to them."

"Sounds like a good way to start," Jack said. "But you should certainly talk to the lawyer who has the original of your parents' will. They may have added or subtracted something recently without letting you know. Chris solved a case not long ago where that happened. And the lawyer may have information in his notes or may recollect something that could be helpful. For all we know, your parents may have told him who was looking for them."

Ariana leaned forward. "I hadn't thought of that. And he wouldn't be able to tell anyone if they were his clients."

"Right."

Her eyes were bright. "I really have to talk to him. The sooner I get that will, the better I'll feel."

I asked her if her copy of the will was in a safe place.

"In a safe-deposit box in a bank. No one besides me has access to it."

"That's good."

"I have some information on the second autopsy," Jack said. "Joe Fox called after you did."

"Second autopsy?" Ariana seemed surprised.

"They couldn't determine the cause of your mother's death in the first one so they got a hotshot ME to come out from the city. His name's Byron Durham and we've been known to refer to him as Lord Byron."

I laughed. "He must be something."

"He is." Jack turned to Ariana. "If you don't want to hear about this, I'll keep quiet."

"I have to hear. I have to know everything."

"It looks as though your mother was chloroformed."

"How do they know that?" I asked.

"Chloroform leaves chemical burns in the nose, mouth, and windpipe and some traces in the lungs if enough tissue is there. It's not easy to detect, which is probably why it was missed by the first ME, who, I'm told, is new to the job. The analysis by Dr. Durham says the chloroform was administered with a pad, sponge, or rag, and he sees the burns inside the nose and mouth."

"Chloroform," Ariana said thoughtfully. "Someone could have held a rag over her face, standing behind her maybe, with his arms around her."

"That's one way it could be done. Nice and clean. No

blood, no bullet, no stab wounds. And when you're ten miles away from the crime scene, you drop the rag in someone's garbage that's to be collected the next morning."

"Was there any jewelry on either body? Anything to identify them?"

"Nothing," I said. "Your father's ring finger showed signs of a ring, probably a wedding ring."

"He wore one, yes. But Mom did too, a thin diamond band that was either white gold or platinum. And she had a diamond engagement ring that she always wore too. She had very thin fingers. Maybe the rings didn't leave a mark."

"And were easy to remove," I suggested.

We talked for a while longer and then Ariana said she wanted to get back to the motel. Her flight would leave early and she had arranged for a taxi to pick her up. I admired her self-reliance, especially at such a time. She promised she would call if she had enough time on Wednesday between going to the bank and getting out to O'Hare airport for the return trip.

In the meantime, I said, I would contact the company her mother worked for in White Plains and see what they could tell me about her.

As she picked up her bag to leave with Jack, Ariana called, "Say good-bye to Eddie for me."

I talked to Elsie that evening, telling her that I might be taking a trip and could she—?

"Of course, Chris," she said, not letting me finish my request. "You know I look forward to your being busy so I get my quality time with Eddie."

"What would I do without you?" I said.

"You'd have a much more boring life—and so would I."

It was true. These detours from the norm filled my life both intellectually and substantively. What I was now involved in was tantalizing; besides the homicides, there was a bereaved daughter who needed answers and didn't know where to look. I hoped the list of former residences and the will would set us on a successful path.

Jack called from New York after lunch on Tuesday to say he knew how to locate phone books on the Internet and we could do some looking tonight. I was glad he said "we." I don't use the computer for much myself, although I have learned how to send and receive e-mail. I was surprised at the number of people I knew who already kept in touch that way. In fact, when I know that Jack will be busy in meetings, I e-mail him instead of calling. Since I count my pennies, I'm always happy to save the cost of a call to New York.

Earlier that morning I had called the White Plains number and reached someone who knew Rosette Parker, the name the deceased used at work and at the bank.

"I'm sorry, Mrs. Parker is no longer with us," the woman said crisply.

"I know that," I responded. "Are you aware that she died about a month ago?"

There was silence for several seconds. "Would you repeat that?" the woman asked.

I said it again.

"Rosette died?"

"Yes. In May."

"That's why she stopped coming to work. We didn't know what to think." The somewhat officious voice softened. "She was always so conscientious, we couldn't understand why she would suddenly not show up. We called her home number but it just rang and rang."

I arranged to drive up and explain what happened. As I was already dressed and ready to go, I alerted Elsie and then I dashed.

I had to sign in and show ID in the building, and then I took the elevator to the third and top floor. Elizabeth Olson, with whom I had spoken, happened to be walking past the reception area as I asked for her, and she led me to her bright, windowed office where I sat in a comfortable chair.

She reiterated her surprise when Rosette had simply stopped coming to work, mentioning clients Rosette had been working with who couldn't believe she had abandoned them.

"She was murdered," I said when I got a chance to speak.

"No!"

I told her briefly how I became involved in the situation, and I watched her face register shock. Then I said, "There are some strange things in Rosette's life that no one is able to explain at this time. I'd just like to know what you knew about her, such as if she had any friends here in the office."

"No, she didn't have friends. She didn't go out for dinner with the others when they got together. She didn't socialize with any of us. Nothing against her, you understand. She intimated she was needed at home, and when she finished her work, she took off."

"So no one here knows her very well."

"But we all liked her. And her clients adored her. I could give you a list of the people she was doing projects for if you think that will help."

"I'd appreciate that. And I wonder if you have the things that were in her office."

"We do. We assumed she'd come back and claim them at some point. Come with me."

I followed her once again, this time to a supply room filled with tall shelves of pads, pencils, pens, diskettes, and all the other paraphernalia of a modern office. In a corner was a locked safe, and Elizabeth Olson opened it and pulled out a cardboard box marked ROSETTE.

"These are all the things that belonged to her. Why don't you have a look? You can sit at a table in the coffee room and take as much time as you want."

She carried the box for me, and I made myself comfortable at a Formica table. I declined coffee, afraid I might inadvertently spill some on the contents of the box. Then I began to go through it.

If I had expected to find an agenda with scribbled appointments and notes about personal things, I would have been disappointed. What I did find was a good-looking desk set with a matching silver pen and pencil, but nothing was engraved on the nameplate. Elizabeth Olson told me that the pads and pencils Rosette used were removed because they belonged to the company. That left very little. A box of Kleenex was the largest item in the box. A bottle of black ink indicated that Rosette owned a fountain pen, although it was not there. The most interesting item in the box was a heavy brown file folder marked PERSONAL in thick black ink. Inside were pages of notes in pencil and ink, along with a few sheets apparently printed from a computer, and the sheets were sorted into groups and paper-clipped together. Each group had a cover page with a name and company on it.

What she had done was make notes and comments to

herself that she could use to ingratiate herself with the clients. In several cases there was a wife's or husband's name, a birth date, a favorite restaurant or food. One client wanted sushi for lunch; another favored pasta.

When I finished looking through the meager contents of the box, I asked Elizabeth if I might take this folder with me, and she said that would be fine. They had already photocopied it. She suggested I take the pen and pencil set as well. I had the feeling she didn't want the company involved in a murder investigation, and if they had nothing of Rosette's, they would be spared. I inserted the folder in an envelope she offered me. Then she scrounged up a plastic bag for the desk set and sent me on my way.

In late afternoon, Ariana called to say she had arrived safely and was packing a larger bag. She intended to be at the bank tomorrow morning when it opened and would go to the airport from there. If all worked as planned, she would be in Oakwood tomorrow evening.

I spent the afternoon calling the people in the file. In every case the person I contacted was shocked and saddened to hear what had happened to Rosette. Eulogies poured out of them. She was such a fine person, such an original and artistic thinker. She was so easy to get along with. Who could have done such a thing?

Not one of them would speculate on the last question. It certainly had nothing to do with business. In that, of course, I was in complete agreement.

On Wednesday morning Ariana called from O'Hare airport to say she had just spoken to the lawyer. "She'll see me tomorrow morning, Chris. Will you come too?"

"Sure. What's her name?"

"Beverly Weingarten. Her office is in lower Manhattan." She told me the address. "Do you know how to get there?"

"Absolutely."

"I made it for eleven. I wasn't sure how long it would take us to get into the city."

"Very good. We'll have an easy trip."

I had asked the lawyer's name so I could call my friend Arnold Gold, who also has a law office in lower Manhattan, and ask if he had ever heard of her. A lot of people practice law in the city, so it was a long shot, but I called him after I hung up with Ariana.

"Yes," he said briskly when his secretary put me through.

"It's Chris, Arnold. And you'll never guess what I'm investigating."

"Hey, do you walk into a room and someone gets shot?"

"Not quite. I have a question to ask you."

"Do I get to decline to answer?"

"Only if you want to. Do you know a lawyer named Beverly Weingarten?"

"As a matter of fact, I do, but not well. She does estate work, not up my alley. I met her at some shindig or other a couple of years ago, and we exchanged cards. A month or so later she sent me a client, someone who had used her services once and now had the kind of trouble she didn't take on. I've returned the favor a few times."

"Tell me what you know about her."

"The clients I've sent to her have been quite happy. I saw something in a law journal not long ago about a case she handled for a couple of feuding heirs. Sounded complicated and sounded like she did a good job. You and Jack writing a will?"

"We did that. I'm looking for the killer of a couple who

lived here in Oakwood. There's a daughter and a lot of complications. Beverly Weingarten wrote the will for the victims. I'm going to her office tomorrow morning with the daughter."

"Well, I'm free for lunch. Give me a jingle if you're available any reasonable time after noon."

"I will indeed."

11

I picked Ariana up at the motel after breakfast and we drove into the city. It was a beautiful spring day, the leaves glossy in that burst of spring newness that I love in the northeast. I gave Ariana a guided tour on the way to New York, which consisted mostly of a catalogue of highway numbers. Driving in lower Manhattan is difficult as it's an area that has more than its share of one-way streets, all running in the opposite direction of your desired goal. However, we found a garage, walked two blocks, and arrived at Beverly Weingarten's building.

Although downtown New York has many buildings dating back over a hundred years, this was a new one, probably built on the spot where an old one had once stood. The elevators were high-speed and divided into local and express. We rode up swiftly, stopped smoothly, and walked less than ten feet to the Weingarten et al. office. After a very short wait, the receptionist led us into a large, sunny office lined with the usual bookshelves. Out a window I could see the East River and Brooklyn. After introductions and handshakes, we got down to business.

From Chicago yesterday Ariana had spoken to the lawyer and explained who she was and why she did not want to be identified by the police. Ms. Weingarten had agreed to work around the problem as far as the law would allow.

"After talking to Ariana, I called Oakwood, and the police faxed me sketches of the two deceased and copies of the autopsies," she said. "I can identify both faces from memory and from the photos they left with me."

I was impressed that the Brinkers had had such foresight.

"At some point you will have to identify yourself to the local police up there, Ariana, and then identify your parents, probably from photos and sketches. If you have any possessions of theirs, like clothing or toothbrushes, that will help make the identification solid. In the meantime, I accept you as their daughter." She pushed a small snapshot of Ariana across the desk. "They prepared me for a meeting like this."

"I see." Ariana was looking unsteady at this point.

"You won't be able to access their bank accounts yet as there aren't any death certificates. They'll be available after the identification is certified."

"I don't need money," Ariana said, not for the first time.

"I don't know your parents' whole story but I know they were concerned that someone from their past might try to injure them, or worse."

"That's true."

"And I know it was their unshakable desire that you inherit all their worldly belongings. I have a list here but I'll hold it until the identification is made."

"May I ask when you last spoke to them?" I said.

"I would guess a year ago. They came in here two years ago to have their wills written, and they called about a year later, just to say they were at the same address and they were still alive and well."

"Did you have my address?" Ariana asked.

"Yes, I did. That's why I asked you over the phone yesterday where you lived. It wasn't a perfect way to determine who you were, but it was a good way to weed out a bungling imposter."

"So you're saying you don't know any more than I do about this person who was after my parents."

"I know almost nothing," the lawyer said. She unbuttoned her dark gray suit jacket to uncover a white silk shirt. She was in her forties, I estimated, with dark hair, wearing a wedding band and diamond ring on her left hand and a watch partly exposed by her shirtsleeve.

"I guess we were hoping you could point us in a fruitful direction," Ariana said.

"Which means?" The dark eyebrows rose.

"Chris and I want to find out who killed my parents."

"I would leave that to the police, Ariana. I'm afraid I have no direction at all for you. But I have an envelope. It may tell you all you need to know." She removed a brown six-by-nine envelope from her file folder. The envelope had several strands of wire around it, and when she laid it on the center of the desk, I saw what appeared to be sealing wax along the flap.

Ariana's eyes widened. "What's that?"

"I have no idea. Your parents brought it in on the day they came to sign their wills. They asked if I would keep it until you arrived to tell me they had died. These wires can be opened only once. After that, they break. You can see they added wax that they left their fingerprints in. No one could duplicate the wrapping. You're the only person I can give this to and you'll have to sign for it."

"OK."

Weingarten pushed a receipt across the desk and Ariana

signed it. "You sign, too," the lawyer said to me. "You're a witness."

I signed and pushed it back. The lawyer handed Ariana the package. "It's yours," Beverly Weingarten said. "I hope it answers your questions."

"Do I have to open it now?" Ariana asked.

"You don't ever have to open it, although I would advise you to do so."

"Then we're finished here?"

"We are. I'd like to see you again after you go to the police. Once there's a death certificate, we can begin probate. You're the executrix. I assume you know that."

Ariana shrugged. "Thank you," she said, rising and offering her hand across the table. She tucked the envelope in her large bag and hung the bag on her shoulder. We were ready to go.

Arnold was still available for lunch and he gave me instructions on how to walk to his office. We set off and I related the origin of my friendship with him to Ariana as we went. I had looked into a forty-year-old homicide soon after I had been released from my vows and left St. Stephen's Convent. In 1950, at the time of the murder, Arnold had been a young legal aid lawyer representing a mentally retarded defendant. In the course of my investigation, I met him and we became fast friends. Now I do occasional part-time work for him. He pays me more than I'm worth, but it's always a pleasure to do something different and have an independent income.

"So you started on a really old case," Ariana said as we neared the familiar old building Arnold's office is housed in.

"That was it. And since then I've been involved in so

many investigations that I think I've lost count. But this one is different," I added, hearing myself say precisely what I had said so many times before. "No one's ever called me and told me a murder was about to happen." I pushed open the door and held it for her.

We rode up in a slow, noisy elevator from a bygone era. When we reached Arnold's office, he was haranguing his secretary gently and looked ready to leave with us or without us. We hugged, I made introductions, and we rode down to the main floor in the elevator that was still waiting for us.

Lunch with Arnold is always a good time. First I tell him about Eddie, then Jack. Then he tells me about Harriet, his wife of many decades, and finally a little something about a case he's been working on that he finds unusual or ridiculous or is memorable in some other way. We went through all this in abbreviated fashion today with no mention of a current case. Then he turned to Ariana and offered condolences.

"But I can tell you, your questions about your parents' murders are in the best hands. Chris has a unique way of looking at things and she edges in where the police are shoehorned out."

Ariana smiled at the metaphor. "The answers may be in the envelope Ms. Weingarten gave me." She dug it out of her bag and laid it on the table. "My parents left this for me. They may have answered all my questions without my needing to lift a finger."

"Then I would advise you to read the contents before you buy expensive airline tickets to far-off places to look for long-lost relatives."

"I will do that, probably when I get back this afternoon."

"In the meantime, let's eat, drink, and be thoughtful."

Which is what we did. Arnold didn't prod Ariana and she occasionally joined the conversation with a comment or personal anecdote of her own. At two, when we were sipping coffee, he glanced at his watch and called for the check. I have learned there's no winning a battle for the check when I'm with Arnold.

"You'll have Harriet and me out one day and we'll let you pick up the bill," he said gallantly, as though we would take them to a New York–style restaurant in Oakwood.

Ten minutes later, we were getting into the car.

I dropped Ariana at the hotel, where she wanted to open the fat envelope in private. She promised to call when she had a plan arranged to investigate the murders, and I assured her that if she wanted to travel, Elsie would be ready on the spot to take over Eddie. I needed time only to pack a bag and make sure there was food in the house for the next couple of days.

She called back at five-thirty, having spent two hours alone with her parents' envelope and her thoughts. She had decided to eat in her room, although she wasn't very hungry after our lunch in the city. There was more in the envelope than a letter, which I had surmised from its irregular bulkiness. In addition to a considerable amount of money, there were addresses and keys and hand-sketched maps. What was entirely missing was an explanation of why anyone would want to murder her parents. Apparently, they did not want Ariana to know, and I found this troubling although I said nothing.

"Besides the personal letter," she said, "there's a letter of instructions. It sounds as though they owned that little house in Madison and they want me to go out there. They have a lawyer to contact right away, and I just talked to him."

"Was he expecting your call?"

"He didn't know my parents had died but he knew he would hear from me when they did. He asked me some questions and agreed I was their daughter. If you think you can leave tomorrow, I'd like to make reservations."

"No problem," I said.

"I'll be paying for these tickets, Chris, and for all your expenses."

"Thank you. That's very generous."

"There's enough in this envelope to cover all our costs. I have no idea where we'll go after Madison, but we can play it by ear as we uncover more clues. It sounds more like a treasure hunt than anything else."

Her next phone call reported our departure time and other necessary information I would leave with Jack and Eddie.

"I would have thought, if these folks were innocent, that they would tell their daughter what the hunt was all about and who the killers were," Jack said in the evening.

"Me too, and I'm concerned. If they committed some felony a long time ago, the killer may have had a rightful grudge, although I don't condone murder under any circumstances."

"Well, maybe there are more answers in the Madison lawyer's office. It sounds as though these people planned very carefully for their daughter to inherit."

"But inherit what?" I asked, not expecting an answer.

"Take a shovel with you," Jack said with a laugh. "Maybe you're going to dig for buried treasure."

* * *

We had adjoining seats on the plane, Ariana in the window seat. Since no one sat on the aisle, I did. We talked sporadically and I showed her the list of Brinkers living in Portland that we had taken off the Internet.

Thinking of the silver anniversary, I said, "Did you ever see your parents' wedding pictures?"

"They had a few, not many. They looked as though they had been taken by a professional photographer, but they weren't in an album and some of them were trimmed."

"Maybe they were removed because your parents didn't want you to see the faces of all the guests."

"I hadn't thought of that." She looked troubled. "That would mean someone at their wedding may have killed them. But you're right, the only pictures I ever saw were of the two of them. No, wait, that's not true. My grandmothers were in one picture and I think maybe a grandfather."

"How was your mother dressed?"

"In a long white gown. And my father was dressed formally, too."

"So it was very likely a big wedding."

"And the killer may have been there," Ariana breathed. "How terrible to think that someone you cared enough about to invite to your wedding would hate you enough to kill you. If only I could get a list of guests."

"Not likely if the killers covered their tracks as well as they seem to have. Did your parents have brothers and sisters?"

"They said they didn't."

"And you never met an old friend from when they were younger?"

"Never."

"Will the lawyer see you tomorrow? It's Saturday."

"He said to call when we arrive today. I think we'll get to come to his office this afternoon. If not, I have his home phone number."

"Your parents certainly found accommodating lawyers," I said.

"They were nice people. Other people went out of their way to be nice to them."

I thought about the wedding, the Brinker-Something wedding. Had they been married in Portland? I supposed we could go from church to church, from hotel to hotel, from restaurant to restaurant, looking for the one that had held the wedding. But old hotels are torn down, restaurants go out of business. Even churches sometimes close their doors when the neighborhood changes and their congregation moves to another part of town. I wasn't optimistic. Maybe there would be answers in Madison.

12

As it happened, leaving New York early had been wise. We arrived at our hotel in mid-afternoon and Ariana called the lawyer before she opened her suitcase. He was waiting for us. We got a taxi and landed at his office about ten minutes later.

Madison is, of course, a college town. It exudes the kind of feeling that has always appealed to me. There's a relaxed atmosphere among the people in the street, particularly near the campus. The taxi driver offered to give us a brief tour, but Ariana said we were in a hurry and he took us directly to the lawyer.

The office was on the second floor of a low building on a commercial street in the heart of the city. The receptionist was expecting us.

"Mr. Keller is waiting for you, Ms. Brinker. Come this way."

The office had a friendly, homey look, a far cry from Beverly Weingarten's lush appurtenances. A graying man in shirtsleeves and little glasses on the tip of his nose rose and came around the desk to greet us. He carried a snapshot of Ariana in his hand and he compared it to the real face for several seconds. "I'm Wally Keller. Glad to meet you, but I'm sorry about your parents."

Ariana made a brief introduction of me and explained she had picked up an envelope from the lawyer in New York, which he had already guessed. There was no other way she could have come upon his name and phone number.

We sat and he offered coffee, which I accepted. I noticed a file folder on his desk that I assumed was the Brinker file. He pulled out a brown envelope, very much like the one Beverly Weingarten had delivered to Ariana in New York, and left it on his desk. It, too, was sealed with wax and wire. We had arrived at step two of the hunt.

"Let me begin by giving you some information you may not yet have. Your parents owned a house here in Madison."

"They owned it in their names?" Ariana said with surprise.

"Through a corporation we set up for them some years ago. I manage the details, provide for maintenance, pay the taxes, and so on. It has been rented to a few professors at the university over the years, and when it was empty for a while, one or the other of your parents would stay in it for a week or two. It's completely furnished."

"Is someone living there now?" I asked.

"Not at the moment, as it happens. The Farrels left for a year in Europe a few weeks ago and gave up the house. You'll be able to visit it without intrusion."

"What's in it that I would want?" Ariana asked.

"I don't know the answer to that, but it's a fine house and it will be yours." He handed her the envelope. "Whatever your parents wanted you to know is in here. When the paperwork is done and you have death certificates, you're free to put the house up for sale, unless you choose to live in it. It's in a nice neighborhood, not far from the campus, and I can tell you it's in A-one condition. By the way, I talked to Ms. Weingarten this morning and she confirmed what you told me on the phone yesterday."

"You had her name and phone number?" Ariana asked.

"Well," he said with a smile, "you may not recall, but you gave it to me when you called yesterday. I had it from your parents, too. I gather she has spoken to the police in the town where your parents died."

"She got as much information as she could from them, including copies of the autopsies. But she didn't tell them I'm their daughter. I'd like to do as much as I can before I cooperate with the police."

"I understand," he said. "I hope you'll keep me up to date on whatever you learn. That's not to say you have to tell me the contents of that envelope. That's yours and yours alone. If you decide to sell the house, I can handle that for you."

"Thank you."

We returned to the hotel, and I decided to go for a walk while Ariana opened the envelope. We were sharing a room and I didn't want to get in her way at a potentially emotional time. It also gave me a chance to make some calls from a phone downstairs. I talked to Eddie, but it was too late to reach Jack at work and he hadn't come home yet. Elsie said she had brought a good dinner with her so that poor Jack wouldn't have to do any cooking tonight. Poor Jack, I thought. It was bound to be the best meal he'd had all week. And if I knew Elsie, there would be plentiful leftovers.

I walked around the hotel lobby, looking in the shops on the main floor, wondering if Eddie would appreciate a sweatshirt from the university. I decided he'd like it very much and went in and picked up a child's size. As I paid for it with my one credit card, a chill went through me. My son might want to go to college away from home. Come on, Kix, I said to myself silently, using my childhood nickname, you're a woman of the world; you have to let him go one day. Just not too soon, I added, taking the bag from the cashier.

I gave Ariana a full hour to absorb whatever information and possible surprises might be enclosed in the brown envelope. When I returned to the room, I knocked and waited for her "Come in" before I slid my key card in the slot.

"Chris," she said. "I don't know how to tell you this. It's very weird."

"What do you mean?"

"It really is a treasure hunt. My parents have buried something on the property they own. Look. They drew a map for me."

The map was done on graph paper to keep the perspective accurate. It showed the rear of the house, the brick patio, the lawn, and the limits of the property. Marked in heavy black ink were a number of bricks in the center of the patio. "Is something buried there?" I asked.

She nodded. "It's all explained in the letter. A long time ago, they hired someone to put in a patio behind the house. They told him they were thinking of planting a tree or putting in a piece of sculpture, so the workmen left this area in the center without a concrete base. Then they buried whatever it is they want me to dig up."

"This is unbelievable," I said. "My husband said I should take along a shovel—"

Ariana laughed. "Did he really?"

"He did. I guess I should have. We'll have to find a hardware store."

"I'm going to rent a car," Ariana said. "Even if it's for just one day. It'll make everything easier, and we can get around the city and back to the airport."

"Good idea."

"Maybe they buried a sculpture. But what will I do with it? And where did it come from?"

"Let's not speculate. It may just be another envelope all wrapped in plastic directing you to another location. How are we supposed to dig up these bricks? Aren't they cemented in? Otherwise the tenants might find them getting loose."

"They're cemented in but Mom says they'll be easy to get up. We'll need a chisel, too. I guess when she visited over the years, when there were no tenants, she checked on whatever was buried there."

"It's too late today. Let's have dinner and set the alarm for tomorrow morning. Hardware stores open early and someone at the desk ought to be able to steer us to one."

Ariana called the desk and ordered a rental car for the next day. Then we went down to the hotel dining room and had a good dinner. I could safely call this the most mysterious trip of my life.

After breakfast on Saturday we picked up the car and drove to a huge hardware store where we bought a hammer, a chisel, two pairs of work gloves, and a spade. Then, using the Brinkers' map, we drove to the house at the edge of the campus.

It was on a beautiful tree-shaded street lined with brick and frame houses as far as you could see. Some must have been rented to students, who were out this sunny morning washing their cars in bare feet and entertaining friends. There were also children scattered around. Ariana drove slowly, looking for the number of our destination. When we found it, she pulled into the drive and stopped in front of a one-car garage. The front lawn was clipped and trees shaded the front of the house and the well-trimmed hedges.

"This is it," she said. "The house I loved so much."

Ariana used one of her keys to unlock the front door. Inside, the house was clean and pleasantly furnished. The kitchen had dishes in cabinets and flatware in drawers. The refrigerator had been cleaned and turned off. The door hung open.

I followed Ariana upstairs, where she wanted to look at the bedroom she remembered so well from her childhood. She walked in and stopped, looking around at the furniture, the windows, and the rug.

"It's almost exactly the same," she breathed. "I loved those curtains. Aren't they wonderful?" She walked over and touched their pristine whiteness. Then she flicked the bedside lamp on and off.

I watched her open the closet door. Hanging on the rod were a number of hangers. Otherwise, the closet was empty.

"Let's go out back," she said, and we left the room. She glanced in the master bedroom and the tiny third bedroom, and then we went downstairs and out the back door. She took the map out of the brown envelope and we stood side by side on the brick patio, looking for the bricks we needed to dig up.

"I'll get the tools," she said, "and put the car in the

garage." She walked around the side of the house to the car. I followed in her wake, opened the garage door, and grabbed from the car the hammer, chisel, spade, and work gloves we had bought.

It was easy to identify the bricks we had to dig up and even easier to raise them with the chisel. They came out smoothly and we set them aside. When they were all out, we discovered a covering made of a stiff sheet of plastic. This we pried up and found packed earth underneath. Ariana took the spade and began to remove the earth, working carefully as though she might injure a piece of glass. She went down several inches and said, "I think I've found something."

We dropped to our hands and knees and pulled away the earth with our fingers.

"Here it is." She reached down and jiggled something black, moving it from side to side to free it. It, too, was encased in plastic. She brushed the dirt away and tried to tear the plastic, but it was strong and didn't yield. I handed her the chisel and she poked a hole in it. From there, it was easy going.

"It's a suitcase," she said, pulling a stiff-sided bag out of the covering material, "kind of like an old-fashioned salesman's bag. And look, it has my father's initials on it in gold."

"I'm going inside," I said, getting up off the brick surface. "You look at it alone."

"That's OK, Chris."

"No. This is your message from your parents." I went inside and sat on the sofa in the living room. If it was old, it had been well cared for. It was firm and comfortable and faced a television set across the room.

I must have sat there for a full ten minutes before I heard the back door close and Ariana call, "Chris?"

"I'm in the living room." I rose and started toward her voice. When I saw her face, I was shocked. "What's wrong? What's happened?"

"It's not what I expected." She dropped into a chair, the closed suitcase on the floor beside her.

"Is it something bad?"

"I don't know, but I think it is."

"You don't have to tell me, Ariana. You don't have to show me. We can go back to Oakwood or you can go anywhere you like by yourself. You have no obligation to me."

She sat back in the chair, her hand covering her mouth as though she were afraid she might speak the wrong words. Her eyes were moist and fearful. Finally she said, "There's money in there, lots of money. And jewelry."

"Is there a letter?"

She nodded. She was holding it in her other hand. "My mother writes that the jewelry came from Grandma Brinker and the money—"

"You don't have to tell me, Ariana."

"She says they inherited some and earned some and it's all mine."

"Was your grandmother wealthy?" I asked.

"My mother says so in the letter. There's even a letter from my grandmother in the suitcase telling me how much she—" She paused. "How much she loved me and how much she would have liked to know me."

"Is there a return address?" I asked.

"There's no envelope at all. She just signs it 'Your loving grandma, Adelaide Brinker.'" She looked desolate, unable to say more.

I had a feeling I knew what was bothering her but I

didn't want to be the one to say it. Walking to the kitchen, I looked out the window for a minute or so, and then returned to the living room. Ariana was sitting just as I had left her.

"What if they stole it?" she said in a voice so low I could hardly hear her.

"You don't know that."

"But that could be the reason—the motivation for the manhunt. Maybe it happened while we lived here, maybe later."

"When did your grandmother die?"

"I'm not sure, but not before we lived here. It's just that it's so much money and it's all in cash." She opened the case and pulled out a rubber-banded stack of bills. From where I was sitting, I couldn't see the denomination, but I could see that they weren't new bills.

"There are a hundred in each batch and they're hundred-dollar bills. I didn't really count, but there could be a million dollars here." She looked at me. "A million dollars, Chris. Is it likely that my father's mother had that kind of money?"

The amount shocked me. People keep saying a million dollars isn't what it used to be, but for me it's so much money I can barely conceive of it, especially in one place— and most especially in the same room that I was sitting in.

"Ariana, I don't know what's likely any more than I know what's true. I know there are people who accumulate large amounts of money in their lifetime. Maybe your grandmother was one of them."

"But what if she wasn't? What if this is stolen money? What if my parents did something awful and this is the result? There isn't a word in any of the letters they've written me about why someone was after them. Why?"

"I can't answer that. But let me say this: You knew them and you loved them. You're a good judge of character. You knew I could be trusted, and you were right. Unless you learn something definite that tells you the money was acquired illegally, I think you should act as though it's yours. But I think the worst thing you can do is make public what you've found. The person who murdered your parents is still out there, and if he hears that the money has turned up, he may come after you."

"You're right. I hadn't thought of that. He may want me dead, too." She got up and closed the curtains, as though the person in question might have arrived just after we did and had been spying on us. When she came back, she said, "Here's what I'm going to do. I'm going to bury this again, just the way it was. We can get those bricks back in place, can't we?"

"Sure. It may be a bit uneven but we can put some lawn furniture over it. No one will be able to tell. Besides, it's your house. No one's coming back to it till you decide to rent it."

She took one pack of bills out and dropped it in her shoulder bag. Then she asked me to help her rebury the suitcase. We went out together.

The suitcase, wrapped in its torn plastic container, slipped easily into the hole. We brushed soil over it till it was concealed, then replaced the hard plastic cover. More earth followed and then we reset the bricks, filling the gaps between them with earth. We decided to return to the hardware store, pick up some mortar, and finish the job. But even the way we left it, it looked good.

By afternoon, we had completed the job, set a heavy table and a heavy umbrella stand over the bricks. We hadn't eaten anything since breakfast and we were both starving. We closed up the house, making sure every door was locked, and drove back downtown to find a place to eat. I was very conscious that in Ariana's straw handbag was ten thousand dollars in cash.

13

We ate lunch, drove back to the hotel, and sat in our room to discuss our next move. I let Ariana know that if she didn't want me along, I would fly home; otherwise, I could continue on to whatever place she had in mind. It seemed to me that answers to many of our questions might be found in Portland, but I wanted her to make the suggestion first.

"This isn't what I expected," she began.

It hadn't been what I expected either. It was as far from that as I could imagine. "What did you think you would find?"

"An explanation, a letter that said, Here's what the problem is, here's what you should do. Something like that. All of a sudden, I think my parents stole a huge amount of money, and the thought is making me sick."

"That's too simple an answer," I said, although I, too, now feared the Brinkers might have been felons.

"I've spoken to two lawyers who knew my parents only superficially. I need to find someone who really knew them. An old friend, a relative. What do you think of starting in Portland and going on from there?"

"I think Portland is a good place to start."

"I'd like to look over this list of Portland phone numbers. And I'd better make reservations. We can leave in the morning."

"That'll be fine. While you're doing that, let me find out what the nearest church is where I can go to mass tonight."

"Oh." She looked embarrassed. "I'm sorry. I didn't think of that."

"No problem." I took my card key and went downstairs. The young woman at the desk was Catholic and knew a church that had an evening mass. She wrote down the name and address and told me how to drive there. I thanked her and went back upstairs. Ariana was just getting off the phone.

"Did you find one?" she asked.

"Yes. I can drive there in ten minutes."

"I'd like to come with you," Ariana said. "If you don't mind."

"I'd be delighted."

I had time to call Jack and explain some of what had happened and where we were going.

"Any buried treasure in Madison?" he asked, surprising me.

"As a matter of fact, yes." I had not wanted to say anything about it in front of Ariana.

"You think they robbed a bank?"

"It's all old."

"And you can't talk freely."

"Right."

"Told you to take a shovel."

"I thought you were kidding."

"Lieutenants never kid. They can't afford it."

* * *

The mass was very pleasing. A group of children sang hymns, their voices sweet and cheerful. Ariana enjoyed it, too. She had told me on the drive over that she was not much of a churchgoer, nor had her parents been, but as she had attended some Catholic schools, the mass brought back happy memories.

We had a good dinner in the hotel. I noticed that Ariana touched her bag reassuringly now and then. It makes a difference when the contents include ten thousand dollars.

When we returned to our room, we looked at the list of Portland phone numbers I had made, and Ariana began to call them. Although I heard only her side of the conversations, I could judge what the responses were. Some were women whose married name was Brinker but they had never heard of her father. One man apparently tried hard to fit a memory to the name of her father but didn't succeed. She mentioned her grandmother, Adelaide Brinker, several times, with no luck. Twice she got off the phone and said, "Answering machine," and moved on to the next listing.

"My parents have died," I heard her say after she dialed the next number. "I'm looking for family. They never told me much about where they came from except that it was Portland."

The person at the other end spoke at some length, and Ariana said she would call back in a day or two, after she arrived in the city.

"Any luck?" I asked.

"This one's a possibility. Her husband's on a business trip but he should be back soon. I guess a lot of people have moved to Portland in the last few years. Many of these people came from somewhere else."

"So I've heard. It's supposed to be a nice place to live, but it rains a lot."

"My mother said that. She said she'd learned early always to have an umbrella handy." Ariana looked nostalgic. "Why didn't she tell me her maiden name?"

"Because she didn't want you to trace her."

"I guess that must be so."

"Have you finished the list?"

"Not quite."

"Keep at it. I'm going downstairs. I'll be back in a while."

There were phones in the lobby where you could sit, and I took one of those and called Jack. "I can talk now," I said when I reached him.

"What's the deal?"

"There's a lot of money buried behind the house in Madison," I said. "A lot."

"And you think they stole it."

"I'm beginning to think that's what all this is about. They stole the money, buried it under the patio behind the house, and came back to check on it when tenants weren't in the house."

"They rented it with money buried outside?"

"You'd never know where. And we put most of it back and replaced the bricks and put a heavy umbrella stand and an outdoor table over it. We're the only ones who know."

"Good luck," my skeptical husband said.

I told him our plans and said I'd call as soon as we got to Portland. "I'll suggest we look at birth certificates," I said. "And marriage licenses. She has the date of their marriage and the husband's last name. That should help. If we can find her mother's maiden name, it may give us another area to check."

"You want me to get in touch with the Portland police and see if Brinker has a record?"

"Sure."

"Can't do it till Monday, so don't forget to call. Don't forget to call anyway. The men in your life miss you."

"Good. I miss them, too."

"Before you go, how much money are we talking about? What's a lot to you is pocket change to some people. Five, six, or seven figures?"

I did some quick thinking as I don't measure large sums of money in my everyday life. "Seven."

"That's a felony."

"Talk to you tomorrow."

With plane changes we arrived in Portland in the afternoon on Sunday, landing in the rain. Ariana had made a hotel reservation and we took a taxi there. When we were dry and had unpacked our toiletries, she found a map of the city and a phone book and started to plan our Monday schedule, figuring out where she might find birth certificates and marriage licenses. She would try the licenses first to see if she could learn her mother's maiden name.

Then we looked through the residential phone book for Brinkers. My list turned out to be fairly complete, so she called back the woman whose husband was on a business trip. Apparently he had just returned home.

"Yes, yes," Ariana said after going through her opening story. "That could be my father. When was the last time you saw him?" She smiled and made notes on the hotel pad, nodding as she listened. "So we could be cousins," she said. "Uh-huh. Uh-huh. Just a minute." She looked away from the phone. "Chris, could we meet this man for dinner or after?"

"Only in a public place," I said. I wasn't going to some man's house escorted by a twenty-three-year-old.

When she turned back to the phone, it occurred to me that I didn't even want this person knowing where we were staying. She wrote an address on the pad and told him we'd meet him there.

"This is a restaurant that has good fresh salmon," she said to me after she had hung up. "We can get there by taxi."

"And let's make sure we take a taxi home, Ariana. I don't want to get into a car with a stranger, even if you're sure he's your cousin."

"You're right. I have to keep my enthusiasm down. I'm glad you're with me. But I have to tell you. He called my mother Aunt Elaine. That was her name, Chris. He knew her. He really knew her."

The restaurant specialized in seafood and featured salmon from the Willamette River. I found myself feeling pleased that this opportunity had presented itself to us. I was three thousand miles from home, in a place I had never considered visiting, and I was about to eat the freshest salmon of my life. Happily, it's a favorite food of mine, which made it even more of a treat.

As we entered the wood-paneled restaurant, a man sitting at a table with a woman stood and came toward us. "Ariana?" he asked, offering his hand. "I'm Nick Brinker."

Ariana was glowing. She introduced us and we went to the table where we met his wife, Jessie, a woman in her thirties and apparently thrilled to meet her husband's kin.

"I've always wondered where Nick hid the Brinkers," she said. "Please sit down and order a drink."

They were both at least ten years older than Ariana, and as I listened to the initial conversation, Nick gave the ages of his parents and grandmother.

"Adelaide!" Ariana said. "I used to talk to her on the phone when I was a child."

"She died a long time ago—ten years, maybe fifteen."

"That would fit. Tell me about her."

"She was just a great old gal. Jessie never knew her, of course. Granddad, who I don't remember very well, made a lot of money in the fishing industry. Not just catching salmon, but the rest of it too—cleaning, packing, shipping it off around the country."

"What happened to the business?" I asked.

"Granddad died suddenly. I mean like that." He snapped his fingers. "One minute he was alive, the next he was lying dead on the floor. Heart attack. I was a kid. All I knew was one day he was gone. They never told me how it happened till I was older."

The drinks come and the menus with them, and we paused in our conversation although I could see how eager Ariana was to get back to it. Finally, with the waitress gone with our orders, Ariana sipped her drink and looked at Nick.

"Please tell me what you remember of my parents."

"Let's see." He drank, put the glass down, and stared across the room. "They were part of my life when I was little. We visited them, and they came to us—not all that often, I don't think, but I knew we were related. And I remember when you were born."

"You do?"

"I remember hearing I had a new cousin, and we went

to your house and brought presents. I remember everything was pink."

"And then what?"

"Well, that's the funny thing. I can't remember the next time I saw you."

"You mean you can't picture the visit or you never saw her again?" I asked.

"I'm not sure. I was a kid, maybe twelve or fourteen, and I didn't think much about babies, but I think it's possible I never saw any of them again."

"But why?" Ariana asked. "Did your parents and my parents have a fight or something?"

He shrugged. "I don't know. They could have. I really can't tell you."

She looked so disappointed, my heart ached. "Do you have brothers or sisters?" I asked him.

"One sister. She's younger. If I don't remember, she won't. But you know, it's possible my mother still remembers."

"Your mother's alive?" Ariana said.

"She's alive but she isn't well. She's in a nursing home. She had a stroke last year and she's not going to recover. Her memory was affected."

"Do you think we could see her?"

"I don't know why not. I'll call them in the morning and set it up. How's tomorrow afternoon?"

Ariana looked at me, as though I were making the plans. "Sure," I said.

"Let's try, OK?" Ariana said.

Nick nodded. "I'll call you as soon as I know. If you're not there, I'll leave a message."

That was the most important thing that came out of our dinner. Somewhere between the salmon and dessert, Ariana asked if Nick knew her family had lived in San Diego, and he said no. That was the end of conversation about his family except that he told us his own daughter was in kindergarten now, and he pulled out pictures to prove it.

"What became of the fishing business?" I asked him during a lull.

"When Granddad died, I was too young to run it and my dad couldn't. I don't really know how they worked it out, but the business got sold and the money went to Grandma. When she died, it went to her children."

"Which would be your father and my father," Ariana said.

"Right. And my father's share ended up with Mom, but the nursing home and all the medical expenses have eaten up most of it. Which is OK with me. Mom deserves the best care in the world."

I wanted to know how much money we were talking about, but I couldn't ask. It was quite believable that Nick's mother's care was very expensive.

In the end, I had come to believe and trust Nick Brinker and was almost ready to accept a ride to the hotel. However, he said he was sorry he couldn't drive us, but he lived in the opposite direction and the babysitter was waiting. Tomorrow was a school day. So we ordered a taxi, which came in less than five minutes, and went back to the hotel.

"What do you think?" Ariana asked excitedly when we were in our room.

"I think he's your cousin. His memories fit in with the facts that we know. I hope his mother can add to it, although she may not be able to."

"That was my father's share of the inheritance that we found in Madison," she said. "They didn't steal it. They didn't take it away from anyone. They got it legally from my grandmother and they put it away for me."

"It looks like it," I agreed.

"Well, tomorrow I'll try to find out what my mother's maiden name was and see where that leads us. We'll have a busy day."

14

She was right about Monday being busy. Nick called after breakfast while we were putting the finishing touches on ourselves to say we could visit his mother at two-thirty. She liked to rest or even nap awhile after lunch so two-thirty would be perfect. He suggested we take a taxi to the home, the address of which he dictated to Ariana.

"That sounds good," I said when she relayed the message to me. "But if you don't mind, I'd like to play the part of the skeptic and go over there myself this morning to make sure the person we're going to see is actually there."

"You could call," Ariana said.

"I don't know who I'd be talking to. Why don't I do that and you look into birth and marriage certificates?"

"OK." She looked disappointed, but I wanted to play this safe. As genuine as Nick had appeared to both of us, he could have arranged with someone to answer the phone and give us the answers he wanted us to hear. I had to keep reminding myself that two people had been murdered and we could not exclude the family as perpetrators.

We took separate taxis from the hotel, having agreed to meet in the room by noon. My taxi drove away from the center of the city and stopped, finally, outside an institutional building that someone had tried to make appear "friendly," in the common parlance. I got out near the front door and went inside to the reception desk.

"I'm Chris Bennett," I said, thinking it was a good idea to give a name up front. "I'm looking for Mrs. Brinker. I'm a friend of the family."

"Let me see where she is now." She smiled at me. "She's having company this afternoon. I'm not sure she can handle two visits in one day."

"Let me just get a peek at her. I know her son is coming later. I can come back with him."

She checked a schedule and called a young woman in uniform over. "Would you show Ms. Bennett to the ceramics room, Jennifer? She's looking for Mrs. Brinker."

Jennifer was a fast walker and we were at the door of the ceramics room in seconds. I could smell the wet clay as we stepped inside. The room was full of gray heads, most of them female, all of them facing the opposite end of the room where an instructor was moving from student to student, murmuring comments.

"Which one is Mrs. Brinker?" I whispered. "I can't tell from back here."

"Second row, second from left."

"I see." The woman was working intently on something I could not see. She wore a smock and her gray hair was carefully coiffed, almost certainly by a professional.

"Do you want me to get her?"

"Thanks, but I think I'll just come back this afternoon with her son. She seems to be enjoying herself. I don't want to disturb her."

I returned to the reception area, and Jennifer headed off in another direction. I left while the receptionist was on the phone and walked a block to a wide street where I was able to find a taxi.

Since I had most of the morning left, I asked the driver to take me downtown. When I got there, I walked around and looked at the stores, finally entering one to buy another present for Eddie. It was a T-shirt with a big salmon flying across the front. At home, I would show him on the map where Portland was and explain about the fish.

I returned to the hotel later that morning and sat in the lobby where Ariana would see me. It gave me a chance to read the paper. When she hadn't returned by noon, I decided to call Jack. With the three-hour difference between the East and West Coasts, it was three in New York.

"I checked with the Portland police this morning," he said. "Ronald Brinker has no record. The guy I talked to dug pretty deep. He had to call me back, but he gives Brinker a clean bill of health. If anything turns up, he'll get back to me."

"So maybe my fears about a robbery were misplaced. And according to what we learned from an apparent cousin of Ariana's last night, a lot of money may have been passed down to Ronald Brinker's generation, the proceeds of the sale of a big business."

"Glad to hear it. I'm sure Ariana feels better."

"She does."

"And you've found a blood relative."

I told him briefly about last night and then of our plans for the afternoon and what I had done this morning, which he liked.

"And Ariana's getting the marriage license?"

"I hope so. She went off more than two hours ago and hasn't—there she is." I waved and she saw me. "I'll talk to you later."

"Hi," Ariana said. "Did you find her? Was she there?"

"Yes to both questions, but I didn't talk to her. I just wanted to make sure I'd recognize her, and I will. She has her hair done, and most of the other women there don't. I didn't really see her face, but she's there. What about you?"

"Well, my father was born here in Portland. While I was at it, I checked out my grandfather, but he must have been born somewhere else. There's no record of his birth. And I don't know Adelaide's maiden name so I couldn't look for her. Then I checked marriage licenses and there they were!" She showed me a copy of the license.

"And there's your mother's maiden name," I said. "Lysaught," I read. "Elaine Lysaught. That can't be a very common name."

"I'm going to check the phone book upstairs. Chris, this may be it. I can't believe it. Let's go up."

When we walked into the room, the phone's message light was flashing. I followed the keying instructions to get into the voice mail and then heard Jack's voice: "Chris, give me a call ASAP. I've got news."

"What could it be?" Ariana said.

"I don't know, but I just talked to him so he should still be there." I dialed his number, wondering what could have happened in the last ten minutes.

"Lieutenant Brooks."

"It's me."

"Chris. I got a call just as we hung up. The Brinkers' vehicle was found."

"I forgot about that. Where did they find it?"

"Ready for a surprise? It was parked in a no-parking zone in Madison, Wisconsin."

"I— Where?" That I couldn't believe what I had heard was an understatement.

"You heard me. Madison, the town you just left yesterday. I'm not clear on whether they found it this morning or yesterday."

"What about the driver?"

"I hate to tell you, but no one stuck around to see if he came back for the car."

"Oh, no," I said, sensing they had missed the best chance we'd had to pick him up.

"They towed the car when they found out it was in the alarms but no one expects it to be claimed."

"I wouldn't think so. Jack, I'd better tell Ariana about this. I'm glad I got you before you went home."

I told Ariana what he had said, and I watched her face change as she listened.

"We have to get back," she said. "Right now. This is terrible. He's after the money."

"Calm down. Let's think about this. Whoever this person is, he or she must have known about the house in Madison, because that's why your parents left it. Over the years he would have had ample time to look for the money if he thought it was buried there. I think the best thing is to call the lawyer and ask that he arrange for someone to watch the house, maybe a security guard from a local company. Although it's probably too late, to tell you the truth. He could have been in and out of it before the car was found."

"But we were there, Chris. We left yesterday. Do you think he was spying on us?"

"Maybe," I said, realizing we could have left a trail that led to this hotel room. "I would have noticed that car if it had been on the street where the house is. It would have had a New York State license plate."

"You're scaring me."

"Maybe because I'm feeling scared myself."

We sat in silence for at least a minute, during which time I reflected on our short trip to Madison. Could someone have seen us pull up to the house and go inside? Could he have guessed what we were doing during the time we were there? If so, the money might be gone by now.

"Let me call the lawyer," Ariana said.

I pushed the phone toward her bed, and she dialed Wally Keller. They talked for several minutes, and it was clear something was amiss. When she hung up, she said, "There's a broken window on the side of the house. A neighbor told the police she thought she heard glass breaking Saturday night, and Sunday morning she walked over and saw the window. The police told Wally and he's having it fixed right now. He said he could send his son over to stay in the house for a while, and I said he should."

"Where did we leave the shovel, Ariana?"

She thought a moment. "In the garage. There were other tools there."

"So if someone broke in and went into the garage, the shovel wouldn't stick out like a sore thumb."

She shook her head. "And we put the mortar on a shelf next to a lot of other stuff, like paint and turpentine."

"OK. I think it's a good idea to have someone in the house for a while. We can think about what to do over the next day or so."

"Right." She took a deep breath, looked at me, and smiled. "Let's have lunch before I drop."

* * *

We arrived at the nursing home on the stroke of two-thirty. Nick was waiting for us in the reception area. He greeted us warmly, and we took an elevator up one floor and walked down a hall to a closed door.

"She knows we're coming," he said as he knocked.

I heard a voice inside call brightly for us to come in. What we entered was not a room but a suite consisting of a sunny sitting room and a pleasant bedroom. The sitting room had what appeared to be Mrs. Brinker's own furniture; there was nothing institutional-looking about it. On the walls were original paintings and on a pedestal was a lovely sculpture, the head of a Greek or Roman god. A fine Oriental carpet covered the floor. This was nothing like the nursing homes I had visited or heard of; it was a private home.

Mrs. Brinker sat in a big chair, a magazine on her lap. "Nicky," she said with a smile. "Now I remember. You said you were coming."

"Hi, Mom." He bent over and kissed her.

She was no longer wearing the smock for her ceramics class. A fresh pink cotton blouse was tucked into a black skirt. There were rings on her fingers and earrings glittered in ears brushed by her shiny gray hair.

Nick made the introductions and gave her time to piece together the relationship. She nodded and looked thoughtful. Then she smiled and offered Ariana her hand.

"You're Ronald's little girl," she said.

"Yes, I am. It's a pleasure to meet you, Mrs. Brinker."

"You mustn't call me that. I'm Aunt June. Everybody calls me Junie."

"Aunt Junie. That's sweet. And you were married to my father's brother."

It took a moment for the relationship to click into place. Then she smiled. "That's right. I'm your aunt. Aunt Junie."

Ariana took the chair nearest her aunt, and Nick and I sat on the sofa. I took out my notebook in case something important came up, but the conversation was mostly about Ronald and his wife. Junie remembered them well, recollected the living room furniture and how nice the curtains were.

"And you were such a darling," she said. "You look just like your beautiful mother, you know."

Ariana smiled. "Did you see much of me after I was a baby?"

Junie shook her head. "I don't remember. And I don't remember seeing your sister either."

"My sister? I have no sister."

"Oh yes, you do, or at least you did. You were a twin, you know."

There was a silence. I leaned forward. "You remember that Ariana was a twin?" I asked.

"Oh yes. We talked about it."

"Did you see her twin sister?"

"I don't remember. Isn't that funny? I'm so sure she was a twin and I don't remember seeing two babies. Well, my mind isn't what it used to be. Nicky, how is my darling granddaughter?"

They talked about Nick's daughter for a while, and then Ariana gently brought her back to the topic of the missing twin. "You remember her name, Aunt Junie?"

"No. It's all a blank. I didn't remember your name either, dear. But there was a twin. I'm sure of that."

Nick said, "Maybe it'll come back to you, Mom."

"Oh, things come back all the time. What did you say your name was, dear?" She looked at me.

"Chris."

"Of course. Chris. And how do I know you?"

"I'm Ariana's friend."

She looked confused.

Nick come to her rescue. "That's Ariana, Mom. She's Uncle Ron's little girl."

"That's right. Now I've got it. She's one of the twins."

"I'm not a twin," Ariana said when we were back at the hotel. "I would know."

"There are things your parents didn't tell you. Maybe that's one of them."

"But what's the motivation?"

"Maybe they just didn't want you to know you'd had a sister who died. There was someone in my family that was kept a secret from me. My parents didn't want me to know. Happily, I met her near the end of her life and was able to have a rewarding relationship with her."

Ariana looked sad. "I'm going to call the Lysaughts," she said. "Maybe someone will remember my mother."

With so few Lysaughts in the phone book, she figured out quickly that none of them was a relative.

15

During dinner, we worked out a plan. In the morning Ariana would check if there were any other children born to her parents. It was possible that the other birth had taken place a day sooner or later than Ariana's. And if nothing turned up, she would see if the hospital had a record of another birth for her mother, perhaps a stillborn child. Neither of us knew where this might lead us but we needed to check it out.

Ariana thought that we should return to Madison and dig up the money, assuming it was still there. Was it possible, she asked me, that a twin could have been given up for adoption and then, angry that her birth parents had abandoned her, eventually killed them?

"It's possible," I said. "If that's the case, you may recognize her as a sister or a mirror image when we find her."

"Maybe she was, you know, deformed or something. Maybe that's why they gave her away."

I know Ariana slept poorly that night. I woke up myself a couple of times and once found her sitting at the curtained window. Another time, she was tossing and turning, small moans escaping her lips.

I tried to think what we would do if the money was gone. There was no record of its existence, and if the killer of her parents had found it and hidden it elsewhere, there was no way she could legally claim it.

In the morning Ariana was up when I opened my eyes. I could hear the hair dryer humming in the bathroom and when she came out, she looked remarkably fresh and well rested. We had an early breakfast, and then she left to look into the birth certificate of the possible twin sister while I stayed behind to call the hospital and see if I could get information over the phone.

Hospitals are tough to deal with when you're asking the kinds of questions I had. I can't say I'm sorry about that; I don't want strangers prying into my past. But it quickly became clear that I had no chance of learning anything on the phone.

We had decided that I would await Ariana's call and then make our plans, so I stayed in the room. Since there was plenty of time, I called Jack, who had no further information. He reminded me that there were laws against carrying a lot of cash, and as we would have it on our person or in our hand luggage, security people might find it when we checked in to fly out of Madison—assuming that the money was still there for us to retrieve. It was something I had thought about, too, but hadn't mentioned to Ariana.

The phone rang shortly after I had talked to Jack. It was Ariana.

"There's nothing," she said. "If there was a twin, she had to be born at some other time. I've checked several days before and after my birthday. I think Aunt Junie got it wrong."

I told her about my call to the hospital. "But they might treat you differently if you're there in person."

"Then let's meet there, Chris. Can you leave now?"

"Sure."

"I'll see you inside the main door, wherever that is."

We found each other easily and went to the records department. I have done this sort of thing in New York, and it's interesting and rewarding to observe the differences when you leave the hurried East Coast and venture west. People just seem so much nicer, much more willing to take a little time to help you. In this case, Ariana was almost a secret weapon. She had such a ready smile, such a kind disposition, that she elicited smiles and kindness from others. Erica, the second woman we spoke to, agreed to go down to the storage area and search manually for information.

In this computer-enhanced age we sometimes forget that earlier in our lifetimes there were no means of computer storage, or, if there were, tapes still had to be located, put into monster machines, and printed out. That ubiquitous screen sitting atop the desk today was just coming into being and so expensive that budgets often could not extend to it.

Finally, about half an hour later, Erica returned from her good deed. "If you had a twin, she wasn't born here," she said, pulling a chair over to join us. "I have a copy of the papers your mother filled out to get a birth certificate for you. I've got your little footprints. There just wasn't another baby born to your mother here ever as far as I can see."

"So that's it," Ariana said. "Any ideas?" She looked at me.

"Not at this moment. I think we should go. We've got to check out of the hotel."

"Right." She thanked Erica and took the copies Erica had made of the papers, and we left.

* * *

We arrived in Madison after dark, having been standby on one of the planes. Ariana rented a car at the airport and we drove to the house even before we registered at the hotel.

Lights were on in a couple of rooms, and Wally Keller's son opened the door at the first ring. "Oh, hi," he said. "You must be Ariana Brinker. I'm Wally Junior." He told us nothing had happened, no one had rung the bell, he hadn't seen anyone lurking in the area.

"But what about the break-in?" I asked. "Was the house disturbed? Was anything obvious missing?"

"There's nothing here to take," Wally said. "Look around. No one's going to take an old TV or used living room furniture. I went through the house when I got here. Maybe some of the drawers upstairs were open slightly, but that's it. In the linen closet, the sheets could have been moved. What were they looking for?"

"I wish I knew," Ariana said innocently.

We all trooped upstairs and went through the bedrooms and bathroom, but they were just as Wally had said. When we got downstairs, Ariana said she would look out back and she could do it alone. I took that as my cue to distract Wally while she inspected the brick terrace.

"Anything missing in the garage?" I asked him.

"Gee, I didn't think to look. I've got my car there. Wanna see?"

I followed him to the small garage and saw the shovel just where we had left it. While I hadn't committed the interior of the garage to memory when we were here, it looked the same. No tools were lying around; everything was neat. I even spied the mortar on the shelf with the paints.

When Ariana came in, she told Wally we would be back in the morning and he could go then. She thanked him for helping out. He didn't seem to mind. The bed, he said, was very comfortable.

We got to the house so early the next morning that I was afraid we would awaken Wally Junior, but he was up and about, eating a bowl of cereal and listening to music on a small radio. We sat and chatted with him till he was ready to go, both of us feeling rather jittery. No one except us—and Jack—knew of the buried treasure, and we thought that was the best way to keep it.

Finally, Wally stripped his bed, stuffed his clothes in a duffel bag, and said good-bye. When he had driven away, we drove into the garage, closed the door, took our necessary tools, and went to the patio. Once again I was grateful that the trees and shrubs formed a natural opaque fence on both sides of the house and in the back. Someone would have to climb a ladder to see over the greenery, and we didn't expect that to happen. Nevertheless, we looked around the backyard carefully before starting our work.

First we removed the umbrella and stand, then lifted the heavy table and moved it away. The bricks looked undisturbed. We both ran our hands over them, and the surface was smooth.

Carefully, we began to pry up the bricks. Ariana had the original diagram her parents had given the lawyer and we followed it as we had a few days ago. It crossed my mind that on that day, we had not known what to expect, and today, we were in the same position.

Ariana scooped out the soil beneath the bricks and nodded as she felt the stiff plastic sheet we had replaced with such care. "So far so good," she murmured.

We wriggled it out, tapped the dust off, and set it aside. The real test was coming. We scooped earth out, both of us working silently.

"It's not here," Ariana said, her voice breaking.

"Keep going. We buried it pretty far down."

"It's gone, Chris. He's taken it. My parent's life savings are gone." She sat back and brushed her eyes with the backs of her earthy hands.

I knelt at the brick edge and kept pulling handful after handful of earth out of the hole. And then I felt something. I looked up at her. Tears were streaking her face. "There's something here," I said.

"There is?" She bounced over, stuck her hands into the hole, and looked up, smiling. Then she dragged the thing up and out of the hole.

It was the plastic-covered suitcase. Quickly, she opened it and peered inside. "Oh," she breathed. "It's here. He didn't find it. It's here, Chris."

"I'm so glad for you."

"Thank goodness. He must have looked through the house and given up. I'm so lucky." She closed the clasps and set it aside, and we began to reverse the process. We took a lot of earth from the flower bed near the garage and used it to fill in the space the suitcase had occupied and to keep the bricks even. When we were finally done, it looked good. We put the table back over the bricks, as it seemed a natural place for it. We pushed the umbrella stand under the table and set the umbrella in its groove. Then we put our tools away, took a final walk through the house, locked it up, and drove back to the hotel.

The room had been made up and we sat in the two chairs, the money-filled suitcase on Ariana's bed next to her straw bag.

"Here's my plan," she said. "We can't carry all this money on a plane, so I'm going to drop you at the airport as soon as we have a flight home for you. Then I'm taking off in the car."

This surprised me. "Where will you go?"

"Somewhere where I can put this money away safely."

"And then?"

"I'm not sure, Chris. I don't think we'll ever find my parents' killers. I know I have to go to the police in your town and tell them who I am, and I have to get back to the lawyer in New York. But I don't know if I'm ready to do those things yet. I have to think."

"We learned a lot, Ariana. There's a killer out there and we almost brushed shoulders with him over the weekend. One important thing we've learned is that he's careless. Driving that car of your parents was stupid. He must have known the police were looking for it. And parking illegally was dumb. I think we can get him, although I have to admit I'm not sure where to go from here."

"Then do it. I'll pay your expenses when I come east to claim my parents' bodies."

"Before we go anywhere, don't you think we should try to find out what's in the car? The lawyer might be able to get us into it."

"That's a good idea." She went to the phone and called him. When she got off, she said, "We can meet him at his office and he'll take us to the car."

So that's what we did. Wally drove us to a station house where we found the car in the police parking lot. Their crime scene people had removed and inventoried everything inside. The police were now holding these items as "vouchered property/crime evidence" in a large property vault in the building. Wally stayed with us along with a

police officer who watched us like a hawk while Ariana
went through everything.

It was quite a haul. Ariana's parents' wedding rings
and watches and other jewelry were in a suitcase. Ariana
picked up and held each precious piece, wetting it with
her tears. Her father's watch was still working and had
eastern time on it. Her mother's, a small, gold wind-up,
had stopped. There were rings and bracelets, a necklace
with a pendant, her father's wallet, her mother's handbag.

She opened the handbag and looked at its contents. The
wallet had about a hundred fifty dollars and some change.
"Her driver's license isn't here. I wonder what he did
with it."

"What about the car registration?" I asked.

"It's not in my father's wallet but his license is." She
showed it to me.

"I'm glad you got these things back, Ariana."

Wally Keller said, "They're not hers yet. We just have
permission to look, not to take. Everything here is evidence and will become part of the case material. These
things must be held here until the DA in Oakwood's
county makes a formal request. Then they'll be returned
to the DA under seal."

"Of course. But she'll get them eventually."

"Eventually is the key word."

What was missing was anything belonging to the killer.
I assumed he had taken a hotel room and brought his luggage there. Since we didn't know his name, we couldn't
find out which hotel he was in or whether he had hopped
on a plane after the car was taken into custody.

We left when Ariana had inspected every last item.
Wally drove us back to our parked car and we said our
good-byes. The next stop was the airport.

* * *

As soon as the plane took off, I began to have misgivings. A girl in her early twenties was driving around alone with possibly a million dollars in a suitcase. I opened the airline magazine and flipped to the map of the country in the back. That made me feel a little better. The distance between Madison and Chicago was not as far as I had thought. Perhaps Ariana was heading home where she had an apartment, a bank, and some friends. I would call her tomorrow to see how she was doing. Meanwhile, I was exhausted. I ate what passed for dinner, closed my eyes, and went to sleep.

16

When I return from a trip, long or short, I try to make it up to Eddie. I know he loves Jack and Elsie, but I can tell that he misses me when we talk on the phone. I arrived in New York very late at night and had a long drive before I reached Oakwood. Jack was as welcoming as I had ever seen him, and for the rest of the night I basked in his hugs and kisses and his warmth beside me.

Eddie was overjoyed to see me at breakfast and couldn't stop telling me everything that had happened while I was gone. I drove him to school and continued to the supermarket to replenish my refrigerator and shelves. Having spent several days being waited on and cooked for, I needed to return to my more normal mode. The early start to the day put me back home before ten with a full day ahead.

Now I needed to gather my thoughts and pass them on to Sister Joseph, the General Superior of St. Stephen's Convent. She is my last resort when I am working on a homicide and I hit a dead end. And it was quite some time since I'd last visited the convent. The school year would now be over at the college, and I would be able to walk the paths I loved, sit in the shade of trees I had watched reach maturity during my fifteen years there, and visit all the wonderful women who had kept an eye on me.

Angela was on bells as usual, and we chatted happily for several minutes before she rang Joseph's office up-stairs in the Mother House.

"Sister Joseph."

That voice cheers and warms me every time I hear it. "Joseph, this is Chris."

"How good to hear from you. How are you? How are the men in your life?"

I went through the required reports and asked questions of my own. "And I saw Arnold Gold not long ago and he sends regards. I must get you all together at my house one of these weekends."

"May I hope for a visit soon from you and those who tag along?"

"If you want just me, I can come tomorrow. If you want one or more of the tagalongs, it will have to be Saturday."

"Saturday then. It's not urgent, is it?"

I laughed. The reason for many of my visits have at least partly been to discuss a homicide with her. "Not urgent, but interesting. Very interesting."

"I will sharpen my little gray cells. Will you join us for our midday meal?"

"Definitely. Eddie will come. I have to check with Jack."

"We'll have enough, I promise."

With the appointment made, I read my *Times* and then sat at the dining room table with my notes. Ariana had given me every name, address, and phone number she had acquired during the trip, so I would be able to get in touch with people if I had questions. I gathered all these small notepapers from various hotel pads and paper-clipped them together. As I did so, I read each name. I recalled I hadn't asked Aunt Junie if she had been to the Brinkers' wedding. I was sure she had; her husband was brother of the groom, perhaps even his best man. If I could only find a friend of the Brinkers, someone they might have confided in, I might begin to see who had wanted to kill them. It had to be someone from their past.

I waited till noon to call Ariana's Chicago number. There's an hour difference in time and I didn't want to wake her. But there was no answer and no machine to take a message.

Eddie and I had lunch together and decided to swim later in the afternoon. At one, I called Nick Brinker's number in Portland. His wife answered.

"Jessie, it's Chris Bennett calling from Oakwood, New York."

"Oh, hi, Chris. You're back home. Did you get everything worked out?"

"Not really. How's your mother-in-law doing?"

"She was real happy to meet you and Ariana. Nick talked to her on the phone after you left. She forgot your name, but she remembered the visit."

"Jessie, could you or Nick find out if she went to Ron's wedding? And does she remember any names of people who were there?"

"I wouldn't count on the names, but I'll have Nick ask. When I call, sometimes she isn't sure who I am. It's so sad. She was such a smart woman until this happened."

"Thanks, Jessie. Nick can call me at home, and if I'm not here, just let me know when a good time would be to call back. Unless, of course, she doesn't remember anything."

"He'll probably ask her when he visits this weekend. She's better in person than on the phone."

So am I, I thought.

When Jack came home that night, he carried with him the final reports about the two bodies in the morgue. No traces of drugs were found in either victim, except for the chloroform in the woman's body. Neither victim had any alcohol in their system and both had been murdered an hour or so after consuming a meal. Since similar food was found in both bodies, we could assume they had been killed around the same time. It didn't tell me much, but at least the last of the information had come through.

About eight o'clock, the phone rang. Jack picked it up and took it into the family room so he could talk sitting down.

"Joe," he said, "haven't heard from you for a while."

Joe Fox, I thought, judging by Jack's many *uh-huhs*. "Sure," he said at last. "She's right here." He handed me the phone. "Joe Fox."

"Hi, Joe. Enjoying the good weather?"

"Well, I'd rather be playing golf but I'm enjoying the little bit of outdoors I walk through twice a day. How are things at your end?"

I hadn't told him about my trip or who I had accompanied. "Everything's fine here. I'm a swimmer, not a golfer, and I've been doing my laps in the afternoon with my son."

"I envy you. Any closer to finding our killer?"

"I wish I could say I was. You'll be interested to hear that I'm visiting Sister Joseph this weekend to see what she thinks."

"Ah, your friend the Franciscan nun whom I gave a hard time to a couple of years ago."

"The very one. I'm gathering my notes and thoughts and suspicions to pass along to her."

"Suspicions?" he asked, homing in on the key word.

"Oh, Joe, it's just a figure of speech. I have nothing and no one in mind. All I'm sure of is that those poor people were killed by someone who knew them many years ago, maybe as much as twenty-five."

"Well, we have some interesting news. I've given it all to Jack, so there's no need for me to repeat it. If you decide you want to have a look, give me a call tomorrow and I'll set something up."

Jack was grinning when I got off the phone. "They made quite a find," he said.

"I'm listening."

"Was there any furniture in the SUV you found in Madison?"

"None at all. There were suitcases and bags of personal items, all of which belonged to the victims. Ariana went through every piece of jewelry—tearfully, I may add—and the handbag and wallets and their contents."

"Well, Joe's got the furniture."

"Really?"

"Probably not all of it, but a bunch. This guy must have filled the vehicle, driven to an out-of-the-way spot, and dumped it."

"My goodness."

"Someone called the police and said there was furniture scattered around on a piece of farmland a few miles from here. He wasn't sure when he had last walked that way, so we don't know when it was dumped. I'd guess around the time of the homicides."

"Hmm."

"Is that a meaningful syllable?"

"It is to me," I said. "Joe said I could look at it—he didn't say what it was—if I called tomorrow. I think I'll take him up on it. So what could have happened to the rest of it?" I wasn't really asking Jack. "You know, maybe he or they rented a U-Haul for a day and filled it with the bigger pieces. People who move around a lot probably don't accumulate things the way Aunt Meg did." Our basement still had cartons of her memorabilia seven years after she had died.

"Good point. You might check the rental places, although if these guys were smart, they got it somewhere else, maybe even in Connecticut. It's not that long a drive."

"I will make some calls tomorrow. And maybe more possessions will turn up in other out-of-the-way places."

"So the case moves on."

"Yes," I said. "It does indeed."

Joe Fox gave me an address when I called the next morning, and I drove up to White Plains to a police property storage depot to look at the Brinkers' furniture. I had made arrangements with Elsie, promising that Eddie and I would swim when I got back.

Joe met me there. It was a large space, a kind of giant lost and found. A uniformed officer led us to an area that was taped off and marked PETER AND HOLLY MITCHELL. It seemed a long time ago that I had thought of the unfortunate couple by those names. Brinker was still my secret until Ariana claimed the bodies.

We skittered under the tape and I began rummaging through the drawers in a nice-looking old desk. It quickly became apparent that anything that might have shed light on the Mitchells/Brinkers had been removed. There were no checkbooks or bankbooks, no paid bills, no letters. I found pencils and pens and paper clips and the kind of generic materials every desk drawer is home to.

In the bottom file drawer, I found several folders, each with a different heading. One was CAR, and in it were records of when the car had been serviced. A quick glance showed regular maintenance. Another folder, marked MIS-CELLANEOUS, contained the expected assortment of unrelated materials. There were pictures of shoes and clothing, a photocopied street map of an area just outside Oakwood, magazine ads possibly related to Mrs. Brinker's work, and several newspaper clippings.

I paged through them and found an article from the local paper detailing a local homicide I had worked on a couple of years ago. My name was underlined in blue ink and my phone number and address were written along the white space on the side.

"Look at this, Joe."

He took the clipping from me and read it, then turned it to see what was in the margin. "Is it possible this is how she knew you?"

"You know as well as I, anything's possible. And I still don't know whether the victim or the killer called me. But yes, this could be the connection. Maybe Mrs."—I stopped myself from saying *Brinker*—"Mitchell read this, clipped it, looked me up, and thought about calling me in connection with her problems. It mentions I'm an ex-nun—people always seem curious about that—and maybe she thought that would make me trustworthy."

"I could have vouched for you," Joe said with a glint in his eye. "Now why do you suppose they would leave that clipping in the desk?"

"For me to find. What was the purpose of calling me in the first place? There was nothing I could do. This may have been a person—or two people—basking in her final success. I've thought several times that if I hadn't left the phone off the hook, we could have lost that phone number when we got back to my house. I'm glad I did what I did."

"Anything else of interest there?"

I went through the rest of the folders but found nothing in any way connected with the homicides. I found no mention of Ariana, not that I expected to. Everything about her was in the Brinkers' memory. "Doesn't look like it."

The night tables had only books and tissues in them. A couple of wooden chairs hid nothing and two lamps were smashed. I really wanted to confide in Joe all I had learned since the last time we'd talked, but I had promised Ariana my silence.

"So it looked like a good find but it produced nothing that adds a lot."

"Well, I appreciate your letting me see this."

"If anything turns up, I'll give you a jingle."

"Joe, someone in that apartment complex saw the Mitchells loading their SUV. Can you tell me who that was?"

"I'll call you when I get back to my office. What are you thinking?"

"I'd just like to talk to them myself. If you don't mind."

"You know me. Be my guest."

I made a small detour on my way home and stopped at the apartment office to see Larry Stone.

"Oh, hi," he said, recognizing me as I walked in. "How'd that turn out? With the daughter?"

"It was very productive, Larry. I wanted to thank you for calling me last week. We made some progress but we haven't turned it over to the police yet. She has some decisions to make. I know this is a long time for you to remember, but did you see a U-Haul or some other rental truck on the premises around the time the Mitchells disappeared?"

He shrugged. "Can't say I did. Was it during the day?"

"I don't know."

"If it was at night . . ." He shrugged again.

"Thanks anyway."

I was beginning to think that the Brinkers had not intended to move at all, that their killers wanted them moved out. If they didn't pay their rent, Larry would come up one day after calling in vain and find they'd left and think they were deadbeats. So why call me and tell me a body would be found? It didn't seem to fit.

At home I pulled out the yellow pages and found a long list of rental companies in the area. I went through them alphabetically, ticking off each when I was told there was no record of a truck or trailer having been rented in the time period I gave them. It had to have been before the day I arrived at the empty apartment. None of the times or truck sizes worked for any company I talked to. All in all, I decided that if the killer had rented anything, it was out of the range of my phone book.

That was it for Friday. I retrieved my son, suited up, and went off for a happy hour of swimming.

17

Our trips up the Hudson River to St. Stephen's are always pleasant. Jack had agreed to join us and we took off after a late breakfast. The scenery never bores me although I've seen it hundreds of times. For this trip, we had a nice day, somewhat cooler than yesterday, perfect for a drive.

I had called Ariana several times since Thursday morning but she had not answered. I was starting to feel uncomfortable about it. She was a single young woman living alone and traveling with a huge amount of cash. Finally, just on the chance that I could pin down her arrival in Chicago, I called the car rental company and asked them to check whether the car rented in Madison had been returned to Chicago. I told them truthfully that the renter had dropped me at the airport and I hadn't heard from her and was concerned about her safety.

The woman I spoke to put me on hold for a long time but when she came back, she said the car had been returned Thursday before noon at a Chicago location. I felt much better at that point, even though I still didn't know where she was.

When we arrived at St. Stephen's, Eddie hopped out as though this place was his second home and started running toward the Mother House. I dashed after him, leaving Jack to come at his own pace. As I reached the main door, a nun came out with Eddie hoisted in her arms. She turned and I recognized Sister Angela, whose telephone room is just inside the entrance.

"Chris, hello," she called.

"Angela, he's too big to be picked up." I gave her a hug as I reached her.

"Angela's my friend," Eddie explained to me as he hit the pavement.

Jack brought up the rear and said hello to Angela.

"Lieutenant," Angela said proudly. "It's so good to see you." Everyone at the convent keeps track of our lives and accomplishments.

We all went inside and made the rounds, touring the kitchen to say hello, then walking over to the Villa where the retired nuns live. Jack has never become completely comfortable among the sisters, having been educated by nuns as a boy. I'm sure he's always a little afraid one of them will upbraid him for a recent misdemeanor.

Finally, I left the Villa and stopped at the chapel on my way to the Mother House. As usual it was quiet and cool. Two nuns sat praying in the second row on each side of the aisle. This was where we were married, where I had come for solace at difficult times, where I hoped I would always be able to come for the rest of my life.

As I always did, I lit three candles—for my mother, my father, and my aunt Meg. Then I sat near the back and did my own praying, happy to be there once again.

Jack and Eddie reached the Mother House a few minutes after I did. We were all to have lunch in the dining hall, after which I would go upstairs with Joseph to discuss the case.

"There she is," I said, leaving my family for my friend.

"Chris, you're here," Sister Joseph said. "Angela didn't tell me."

"We were visiting. How are you?"

"Very well. My big news is that I am to go to Rome this summer."

"Joseph, how wonderful."

"It's been the dream of my life. I feel well rewarded. That isn't young Eddie, is it? He's almost as tall as I am."

It was a large exaggeration but he had put on a couple of inches since our last visit. After hellos, we went to the dining room and sat at Joseph's table. The nuns stopped one by one at the bank of drawers in the outer room to pick up their napkins and any spices or salt substitutes they happened to need with meals. It struck me once again as I watched them that the average age was increasing, that I was one of the youngest people there besides Eddie. Even Angela was now in her thirties.

It was a fine lunch with home-baked cake for dessert. Most of the nuns came by during the meal to say hello and talk to Eddie. I hoped that when he became an adolescent, he wouldn't reject these visits and the wonderful women who made them so enjoyable.

Afterward, Jack and Eddie and a couple of nuns took off with the baseball equipment Jack had brought along, and Joseph and I climbed the stone stairs to the second floor and walked to the end of the hall where her office was.

Like Joseph, the office never changes. A long conference table fills the front half, and her desk, cabinets, and other necessities find their place at the rear. She sits with her back to a large window that has a beautiful view. This always surprises me. I would prefer the view, but perhaps she's afraid of being distracted.

"Our usual places?" she said as we entered.

"Sure." I moved to what has become my side of the long table, at the far end near her desk.

"Your family looks wonderful," she began.

"Your trip to Rome sounds marvelous." She had described it during lunch. "I'm so glad you're going."

"Well, you got to see the Holy Land. Now, between us, we will have seen much of what's worth visiting in this world of ours."

We sat and I dug out my notebook with all the extras clipped and stapled to pages. On her side of the table were the usual well-sharpened pencils and a stack of unlined paper. I looked across the table and saw she was waiting for me to begin.

I doubt there have been many people who have received the kind of phone call that started everything off. Joseph reacted as I read the dialogue from my notes.

"This woman wanted to tell you of a murder that had happened or was about to?" She sounded incredulous.

"That's what she said." I told her about the empty apartment, the small bloodstain, the weeks of nothing happening, the finding of the woman's body.

I pulled out the sketches of the victims and let her look at them. She smiled and ran her fingertip over the nail polish. It seemed to be the thing that everyone did. I went on about my search for the manicurist, the bank, the pharmacy. I talked about Gladys, the dear lady I had found in the last pharmacy, the one who had ridden in the big vehicle with them on several occasions.

And then there was the arrival of Ariana.

"Their daughter," Joseph said.

"Yes, with a strong resemblance to her mother."

"It took her a long time to check up on her missing parents."

I explained where she lived, how there was no way to leave a message.

"They kept their existence known to as few people as possible," she said.

"So we have learned. I haven't even been able to leave a message for her in Chicago. No machine picks up." I continued my tale: our visit to the lawyer in New York and then our trip to Madison, Wisconsin.

Joseph listened in obvious amazement as I described the letter Ariana retrieved from the lawyer Wally Keller and our drive to the house her parents owned. When I said the amount of money we found, she drew in her breath.

"And you left it there?" she asked.

"We had no choice. We wanted to fly to Portland, where her parents had been married and lived for a while. We couldn't carry it on our persons."

"I would think not."

My travelogue continued: our discovery of Nicholas Brinker, Ariana's first cousin, and our subsequent meeting with his mother. Then I mentioned the missing twin.

"Ariana had a twin," she said reflectively. "If that's true, how can you be sure you talked to the one who lived with her parents?"

It was a question I had asked myself after I returned from our trip. "You're right, that's a potential problem. Even DNA couldn't tell us which is the real one and which the imposter. I know that it wasn't Ariana's voice I heard over the phone the day I got the original call, but I have to think that if the Brinkers knew there was an identical twin around, they would have worked it out to make sure the imposter didn't inherit their estate."

"The imposter," Joseph said with a smile. "The good twin and the evil twin. How would parents know when they were infants that one was evil?"

I gave her Ariana's explanation that perhaps one was born deformed in some way and given up at birth.

"Do you believe that?"

"Not really. There's also the chance that they were fraternal twins. The word 'identical' was never mentioned."

"Perhaps because this aunt's memory is faulty. Go on with your story."

I could sense that she was as uncomfortable with this development as I was. "Another reason I think Ariana is genuine is that if she weren't, she wouldn't have wanted me along on the trip."

"Yes, I see that. The so-called imposter would just want to find the money and run with no one knowing that it existed. Of course, you haven't been able to reach her by telephone. She may, indeed, have decided to disappear."

That troubling idea had certainly come to mind in the last two days. I finished the narrative, pointing out that according to the rental company, the car we drove had been returned in Chicago.

"So you know she got that far."

"Or the car did," I said. "Yes, I believe she got that far. And I would suppose she's opening accounts in banks where she can rent boxes to stash the money."

Joseph began her questions with the phone call I had received. Could I have spoken to Mrs. Brinker in the past and not known it?

It was possible, I admitted.

"I rather think that call to you was staged, Chris. I think

the murders had taken place and the killers wanted to set in motion the discovery of the bodies in order to recover the money you found in Wisconsin."

"They didn't get to Wisconsin till about the time we did."

"Because the killer or killers didn't know where the money was. They were waiting for you and Ariana to make a move. If they had been able to get the Brinkers to tell them, they would have left for Madison as soon as the Brinkers were dead. But the Brinkers died without saying anything.

"The killers knew there was a daughter and assumed she would go for the money. They had to bring her out of hiding, or wherever she was. If you investigated in your usual way, the daughter might surface more quickly. That's why they called you."

"So they waited around till the bodies were found and Ariana turned up. That was a long wait."

"If they had waited twenty years to capture their prey, another week or two couldn't have made much difference. The woman who called you—and I'm quite sure it was the killer, not the victim—wanted you to react. By the time she called, she and her accomplice had emptied the apartment of furniture, perhaps dropped a bit of blood in a conspicuous place, and dumped the bodies where they were sure they would be found quickly."

"But they weren't."

"One can't always judge these things accurately."

"So I was watched," I said, realizing that my family might have been in danger. I knew no one had parked nearby, as all the people on our street use their driveways and garages. Anyone parked at the curb is a guest or is making a delivery, and overnight parking isn't allowed. But there are places as close as a block away where a parked car would not rate a second glance.

"I understand your concern."

"And when we drove to the airport, they followed and found out where we were going and took off after us in the Brinkers' car. I'm sure you could reach Madison in a couple of days if two people alternated the driving."

"Or overnight. They could have been there the next day, Chris. These are resourceful people. They could have found you by calling hotels. How sure are you that no one saw you dig up the money?"

"Quite certain. We pulled the car into the garage and went out back through the house. It's completely private back there. The trees and shrubs are old and thickly grown. And the proof is that they searched the house itself but didn't dig in the backyard. They expected to find something indoors, maybe in the basement."

"Or they were stopped before they could look outside."

"Possibly. A neighbor heard the window break."

"And the police were called."

That explained the known facts. "They probably didn't follow us to Portland though. Also their vehicle—the Brinkers' car—was found at an illegal parking spot and towed. This is distressing."

"And I gather no one has any idea where they are right now."

I shook my head. "What you're saying then is that all this is about money." Somehow, I have never quite grasped that people might kill for money, even such a large sum.

"Not at all," Joseph said, surprising me. "As we talk about it, I think the money may be part of it, but I believe there's something much deeper, much more important going on here."

· I looked at her, not following. "You think this rampage will continue? You think they're after Ariana?"

"They may be. And if she senses these people are hunting her down, that may be the reason why she hasn't answered her phone."

"I see. I wish she would call, just so I know she's all right."

"I expect you'll hear from her, Chris. I think her desire to bury her parents properly will outweigh her other concerns. When she feels safe, she'll come east and formally claim their bodies."

I felt Joseph was right. "And she'll have to see the New York lawyer again, although I suppose all that can be done by mail these days. My sense was that there's more of an estate than what was buried in Madison. There may be bonds or money put away. At least that was the impression the lawyer gave."

"May we go over what was found in that vehicle in Madison?" Joseph said.

I had a detailed list of what we had seen, including the contents of Ariana's father's wallet and her mother's purse. I went through it, mentioning the pieces of jewelry.

"Did Ariana think any of her parents' jewelry might be missing?"

"She didn't say. It was a very emotional time, Joseph. I watched her touch each piece. She talked about some of them. When she eventually takes possession of all that, she may recall some things that are missing."

"You said something about her father's driver's license being there but not her mother's."

"That's right. I don't know why. Her mother had a license. She was the one who drove them to work in the morning."

"Yes," Joseph said. And again, "Yes."

"You see something I don't see."

"I am thinking something you may not have thought of," she corrected me. "There's so much we don't know. And even if we identify the killer, how will we know where to find him?"

"We've been going back and forth between one killer and two. Do you have a sense of how many people are involved?"

"I'm sure it's two and I believe one must be a man, simply because of the strength involved in moving the bodies. I don't know whether these two are husband and wife or perhaps a hired killer and his employer, but they followed a plan. They could have left the bodies in that apartment—the neighbors would have known in a couple of days that something was amiss—but the police would have handled it and you might never have known about it. This way you were in on it from the start; you felt committed because of that phone call. If it hadn't been for you, Ariana might have gone to the police and the killers could have lost track of her. They wanted to know what she would do when she found her parents missing or dead."

"She might not have flown to Madison if she was by herself," I said. "She was anxious for company. By involving me, the killers made sure she'd feel confident enough to go to Madison."

"Exactly."

"So where does that leave me?" I pointedly asked the most important question.

"I suggest you try to find someone who was at the

Brinkers' wedding and see what they know of trouble in the Brinkers' lives at that time and why they fled Portland for San Diego a couple of years later. And I'm going to say something about which I'm not entirely certain, but almost: I don't think Ariana had a twin or even a sister who was not a twin. I think your Auntie June or Aunt Junie is confused and may never come up with the facts you need. But don't give up trying. There have to be other sources."

"I should hear about that soon," I said. I sensed we were done. My papers were lying in the center of the table and Joseph had put her pencil down. I pulled my notes toward me and clipped them in my notebook. "Is that it?" I asked.

"One more thing. Think very hard about why Mr. Brinker's car papers were in his wallet and Mrs. Brinker's weren't. There may be something there."

I wrote it down, fearful of forgetting. "We'll put our heads together," I said, meaning Jack.

"And now that we've talked about your problem, I'd like to tell you about ours."

"A problem?" A chill passed through me. "You're well, aren't you?"

"I'm absolutely fine and expect to remain so. But the convent is in deep trouble, Chris. I've mentioned this before. It's like a cloud that you hope will pass you by, but I don't see how we can ignore its presence any longer. Our novices are almost down to zero. Our average age is close to grandmotherly. I'm young and I'm in my fifties."

I nodded. Each time I had visited I had noted the age of the nuns and the lack of new blood. Each time I returned home, I prayed that the situation would turn around. Joseph had alluded to this problem before, but I sensed that she had now moved from worrying about it to considering solutions. I did not want to hear her proposals.

"I know how painful this is for you," Joseph said, "but we have to consider what will become of St. Stephen's, and I would rather design the solutions than be forced to accept someone else's."

"And what are you proposing?" I asked in a fragile voice.

"We can leave St. Stephen's and join another Franciscan community as a group. We can join other convents individually. We can invite another group of Franciscans to join us."

I let the tears roll down my cheeks. I hated the first two proposals so much I could not bring myself to comment on them. I disliked the last one, but recognized that it was the best. "The college," I said.

"The college is perhaps the bright spot in this mess. Do you know that girls are now looking for all-female places in which to study? Styles change, for which we must sometimes be thankful. What was it Tennyson said? 'Lest one good custom should corrupt the world.' We are working on beefing up some of our departments to draw more bright young women as students. The day may come when I'll call on you to teach a course."

I smiled through my tears. "Of course I would, Joseph. With great pleasure."

"But we need more nuns to keep the convent going. I am in negotiations, if you want to call it that, with several convents in the eastern half of the United States. I don't know if anything will work out. But you'll be the first to know if there's happy news."

"I'm glad there are possibilities. I can't imagine this place becoming a condominium."

"We will try to avoid that. Although I must tell you, we have had feelers from a Protestant church in the area, wondering if we are thinking of selling."

I swallowed and said nothing.

"Why don't we go downstairs and play some baseball?"

18

I was very quiet on the drive home. While Joseph had sounded optimistic about the outcome of St. Stephen's problems, I thought only of the possibilities that the nuns might be scattered about the country or might be forced to join another convent, one in better financial shape but somewhere far from here. At various times I have visited convents in metropolitan areas, and the convents are generally situated in parts of the cities where trouble is a constant companion. That St. Stephen's owned the most beautiful piece of land I had ever walked on was always of great comfort to me. I had felt safe there, never looked over my shoulder to see if I was being followed. We had been as close to a family as any group of unrelated women could be. But it was not all bliss. Some women were overbearing or distant or troubled and thus difficult to get along with. Still, we all tried.

As Jack turned in to Pine Hill Road, I dismissed my thoughts and looked back to Eddie, who had been quietly busy with puzzles or toys during the drive.

He looked at me and gave me his warm smile. "Can I have a cookie now?"

"Let's wait till we're inside and I can pour you some milk. Did Sister Dolores make them for you?"

"Uh-huh. I like her cookies but she kisses me too much."

Jack laughed. "Count yourself lucky, my boy. Those are the sweetest ladies you'll ever meet."

There was a message on the machine. I hoped it would be from Nick Brinker, but it was from Jack's mother. He called her back and spent a while talking before handing the phone to Eddie and then to me. Finally, Eddie and I dashed out for a swim.

The call from Nick came about seven. He had just returned from an afternoon visit with his mother and he sounded low. "She had some kind of episode last night," he said. "The doctor came but he didn't think she needed hospitalization."

"I'm sorry to hear she's unwell."

"I stayed with her a couple of hours today, but she's really out of it, Chris. It took a while till she accepted that I was her son."

"That must be very painful."

"Yeah, it is. I liked it a lot better when she was bossing me around."

"I'm glad Ariana got to see her while she still had some memory left."

"You know, I gave it a try anyway. I waited till she was calm and we were talking about nice things. She didn't even remember that Ariana came to visit."

"That's OK, Nick. It was so nice of you to try."

"Anything we can do to help?"

"I'd really like to know who went to your uncle and aunt's wedding. I'd like to talk to someone who remembers them from that time. It was only twenty-five years ago."

"Hey, I'll tell Jessie to give it a try."

* * *

Jack and I talked later about the problems at St. Stephen's. He commiserated but had no helpful suggestions. He remarked that although such events had been occurring more frequently over the last century, he understood that when it happened to my convent, it was a personal catastrophe. I was glad he understood.

The next day Ariana showed up.

It started with a phone call from the motel. I drove over and picked her up. Jack was cooking dinner, so there would be lots to eat.

"I hope you weren't worried," she said as we approached the house. "I didn't answer my phone and I've moved."

"Just in the last few days?"

"I have a friend who had a bigger apartment and she decided she couldn't afford it. We traded."

I laughed, thinking that being young and single meant you could manage almost anything. "So you have a new phone number."

"Well, I will when I get back. Has anything happened?" She sounded as though she expected a quick no.

"Some of your parents' furniture was found abandoned."

"Really? Have you seen it?"

I told her the story, including my discovery in the desk of the article about me. "So we have a good idea now why I was called." I parked in the driveway and we got out of the car and went inside. After the hellos were over, I poured us some lemonade and we sat under our umbrella behind the house in the light breeze.

"We couldn't have done it here," Ariana said looking around.

"Done what?"

"Dug up the backyard. It's much more open."

"You're right. We would have had to sneak in at night."

"I put it away," she said, and I knew she meant the money. "And the reason I'm here is that I've decided to tell the police who I am and claim my parents' bodies."

"I think that's a good idea. We know the detective on the case, Joe Fox. He may be willing to drop over tonight or tomorrow and talk to you."

"That would be great. I hate the idea of sitting in some kind of interrogation room in a police station."

"Ariana, that's not going to happen. You're a survivor, not a suspect. I'll ask Jack to give Joe a call. Once you've identified yourself, I'm sure he'll let you see the furniture and its contents. It's being stored in White Plains."

I then told her the rest of the developments, especially the call yesterday from Nick Brinker.

"So Aunt Junie's a lost cause," she said. "Well, I told you in Madison that I don't think we'll ever find this killer or these killers."

"Don't give up. Ariana, you mentioned at some point the wedding pictures of your parents."

"Yes. There were several, but not in an album, although some of them looked as though they might have been torn out of one."

"And some were cut."

"Yes. The way you might cut out a picture of your old boyfriend standing next to you."

"Someone was at that wedding who they didn't want you to know about. Nick's wife is going to see what she can find out. Something must have happened between a guest at the wedding and your parents. Do you still have those pictures?"

"I never had them. Mom kept them in a drawer somewhere. If you didn't find them in their furniture, they may be lost."

"Or taken by the killer. Only some of the furniture was recovered, but the desk was there."

"They probably destroyed what they didn't want found."

I agreed. "Why don't we go in and tell Jack you'd like to talk to Joe Fox? I'm sure he can take a little time off from his cooking to make a phone call."

"How did you manage to find a man who would cook for you?"

"I was just lucky. Or maybe he tasted my food and decided he had no choice."

"Does he have a brother?"

We both laughed and went inside.

I knew Jack would be relieved that she was coming forward. It wasn't his case and he had promised his silence, but his conscience was surely bothering him. He called Joe, who agreed to visit this evening for what Jack told him would be a meeting with an important person in the case. I dashed out at that point to pick up something sweet to serve with coffee, leaving Ariana behind to help or get in the way as she pleased.

When Joe arrived at eight, he was as surprised as I had ever seen him. "The Mitchells' daughter?" he said.

"The Brinkers' daughter," Ariana responded, shaking his hand. "Ronald and Elaine Brinker's daughter."

"You've been holding out on me, Mrs. Brooks."

"*I* have been holding out, Detective," Ariana said. "I agreed to talk to Chris only after she promised that she would not tell the police about me. And she was true to her word. We have a lot to tell you."

And we did. At Ariana's insistence, she and I had agreed beforehand not to mention the money. It was rightfully hers unless we learned it had come to the Brinkers illegally, which seemed less likely now than when we initially heard about it. I could tell that Joe had suspicions he didn't voice about why the vehicle had been driven to Madison. He, of course, had heard about it when Jack did, so it was no surprise. The surprise was that we were there, too.

She told a good tale. At times she looked my way for a detail, but for the most part, it was her story. She mentioned the missing wedding pictures, telling Joe my theory that someone at the Brinker wedding had had a falling out with them a few years after they were married.

"But you still don't know what that's all about," Joe said.

"No, we don't," I said. "I have someone out there working on it, but I'm not hopeful. There don't seem to be many identifiable people around who attended the wedding."

"But I'm sure it was a big wedding," Ariana said. "Mom was wearing a long white dress and Daddy was in a tux. You don't do that for a wedding in the minister's study."

"Well, we'll see what we can find out. I'll have to ask you to drop by our office tomorrow so we can formalize what you've told me."

"I will. And whatever I have to do to get my parents' bodies released . . ."

"We will get that moving. I'm sure that's important to you."

Later, after Joe had left, we sat quietly in the family room.

Ariana appeared deflated. She had come to terms with her parents' death, with the fact that they were murdered, very likely by someone who knew them, who was part of their inner circle a quarter of a century ago. Jack drove her back to the motel and I dug out our wedding album. I hadn't turned the pages for a long time but I wanted to get some idea how the formal pictures were set up—who might have stood beside the bride or groom.

I viewed the pictures slowly, relishing the images. I was a bit thinner there and looked younger, which startled me. But the changes in Jack were more pronounced. He still had a head of curly hair at that time and he seemed even more like a big kid than he did now. The hair has been trimmed and his face has taken on some of the cares that are part of his daily life. In short, we have aged.

What I realized, not for the first time, as I flipped the pages, is how different my family situation is from most people's. I was orphaned in my mid-teens so there were no parents in the wedding pictures. I am an only child, so there were no siblings. I lived half my life in a convent, so the people nearest and dearest to me were nuns. Several pictures showed Jack and me with groups or tables of Franciscan nuns. Not your ordinary wedding pictures.

Who might have been cut off from the Brinkers' pictures? A best man, a maid of honor, a parent, a sibling? How could we possibly figure out which of those it was without speaking to someone who had attended the wedding?

Jack returned as I was finishing my nostalgic journey. "That our wedding album?"

I told him why I had gone through it.

"Let me see." He flipped to the beginning, chuckling as he turned the pages. "I look like a kid," he said. "How could a mature woman like you marry a kid like that?"

"You showed great promise."

"And?" He turned to me.

"You've fulfilled it."

"Yeah." He stopped at a portrait of the two of us. "You are one gorgeous woman, do you know that?"

My eyes filled. "Thank you."

"Just speaking the truth, my love." He closed the book. "Let's go up. This has stirred all kinds of marital longings."

It had in me, too. I put my arms around him and we hugged. Then we went upstairs.

19

I drove Ariana to see Joe Fox at the sheriff's office the next morning. I waited in a hard chair while she went inside to give her statement. It took longer than I had anticipated and I regretted having said I would wait. At least the dentist's office has magazines to read; here there was nothing. I got up several times just to use my muscles, and I went to the watercooler but the water wasn't cool. Finally, after more than two hours, a wilted Ariana walked out, Joe Fox trailing her.

"What's wrong?" I said, getting up. "You don't look so good."

"He thinks I killed them," Ariana said.

"I never said that, Miss Brinker. I said you know a lot more than you're telling me." He sounded as annoyed as I had ever heard him, and he didn't speak to Ariana with the deference he had used with Sister Joseph.

"We'll get you a lawyer," I said crisply. "Let's get out of here."

"Mrs. Brooks, I am doing my job."

"I know you are, Joe, but you're doing it wrong. And she should have a lawyer. Come on, Ariana." I took her arm and led her out of the building.

As we set foot in the parking lot, she began to cry. "I

thought this was just going to be a statement. He harrassed me. He said I was lying. He kept asking me about the house in Madison—why I went there, who I met. He thinks I had an accomplice who drove my parents' car there the day we flew."

"He's lost his mind," I said angrily. "He can't put you anywhere near the murders. He'll never find your prints in your parents' car. Did you leave any in the apartment?"

"When I came looking for them, I'm sure I touched things."

"But they lifted prints long before that. We'll call Arnold Gold as soon as we get home. You've already spoken to him. He'll be delighted to represent an innocent person. And you can trust him. Unless you have another lawyer in mind."

"I don't. The only lawyer I know in New York is the estate lawyer."

"How dare he," I said.

"You're really angry. That makes me feel good. You believe me."

"Of course I believe you. I went to Madison with you. I went to the estate lawyer in New York with you. I know why you went to Madison. Listen, if Joe had the slightest amount of evidence, he'd charge you. He has nothing."

"Maybe he thinks I know who did it and I'm protecting him."

"Well, if you do, you can save yourself a lot of trouble by telling Joe Fox."

"I don't, Chris. And I don't know why they were killed unless it was because of the money. And I feel terrible."

"He'll probably come after me next for a statement," I grumbled.

"He said something about that. I think he was going to ask you, but we stormed out of there."

"Good. He can tell Jack I'm withholding state's evidence." I was in a fury. "Is he going to release the bodies to you?"

"He said he would, but not just yet. He'll have their death certificates issued. At least he's convinced I'm their daughter."

"Then he got one thing right. Did you have your birth certificate with you?"

"Yes. He made a copy. He asked something that I think got me in some trouble."

My heart did something funny. "What was that?"

"He wanted to know where I worked. I told him about the bookstore, and he asked if there was anyplace else. I used to work for a drugstore in Chicago, just part-time behind the counter. I'm not a pharmacist."

"Did he tell you why he asked?"

"To see if I had access to chloroform." Her voice shook. "My mother was killed with chloroform. He thinks I stole chloroform last year and saved it to kill my mother."

She asked to go to the motel and I dropped her there. "Do you have your bill from the last time you stayed here?" I asked as she was getting out of the car.

"Yes. Why?"

"Any phone calls you made would be on it. So if you called your accomplice, there'd be a record."

"I'll find it," she said. "I'll call you later."

As I drove home, it occurred to me she could have made calls from the lobby, as I had when we were in Madison. Well, let the sheriff's people get to work and check out every call made from the lobby during the time of her first visit.

I called Arnold and caught him before he left for lunch. He groaned when I explained what had happened and assured me he would represent Ariana. Then I sat down and tried to think what had made Joe Fox suspect her.

If she had an accomplice, her ability to prove she was in Chicago at the estimated time of the murders didn't matter. In fact, she would have arranged to be there. She had a key to the Brinkers' apartment, which she could have copied and handed over to the killer. Apartment keys were easily duplicated in any hardware store. She knew many of her parents' secrets and could compromise them. She knew where her parents worked and might even have a key to their car.

All of that had to do with means and opportunity and, taken together, it made me uneasy. But what would be her motive? From Joe Fox's point of view, the Brinkers might have a ton of money stashed somewhere, perhaps legally in banks and locked boxes, and she wanted it. And since he had no idea that I had been with her when she uncovered the suitcase, he wouldn't know what a surprise the find had been. To me it seemed unlikely that Ariana would have uncovered that treasure in front of me if she knew what she was digging up. Even if I had been sworn to silence, she would suspect that under oath I would tell the truth, given that I was asked the right questions.

But Joe Fox knew nothing of this. He had two dead bodies, a daughter who hadn't turned up for a few weeks after they died, and then, when she did, she had snubbed her nose at the police.

Last night, Joe Fox had given me the name and apartment number of the person who had seen the Brinkers loading their SUV. I telephoned the number, got an answering machine, and hung up. I would go over there tonight.

I called Jack and told him what had happened.

"You know, the pressure's on Joe to close this case. He has no one and then a daughter shows up. Why didn't she come forward sooner? If she had some guy working with her, she didn't have to be there. He can find all kinds of reasons to consider her a suspect."

"What's your take on it?" I asked bluntly.

He didn't answer for a couple of seconds. "I don't think she did it, Chris, but I've been wrong. I think Joe's a damn good detective, but we've both seen him make a terrible mistake before. I would believe Sister Joseph over almost anyone else I know, and he gave her a hard time when that girl got killed a couple of years ago. Still, he can't let Ariana off the hook just because she seems like a really nice young person who's lost her parents."

"She worked for a pharmacy, Jack, a year or so ago."

"Shit."

"Why would they use chloroform on one and a gun on the other?"

"Chloroform's quiet and, as we've seen, sometimes undetectable. A strong guy could hold her mother down, but whether he could do the same with her father is questionable. And then there's the question of noise. The killer may have come prepared to use more than one method, depending on the circumstances. He'd rather do it cleanly and quietly."

I heard shouting at his end. "Gotta go." And he hung up abruptly.

Before Eddie and I left for the pool, I called Ariana at the motel. "Will you join us for dinner?" I asked.

"I don't know," she said in a lackluster voice. "I'm not feeling very up."

"It's your choice, Ariana. We'd love to have you."

"OK, yes. Thanks. You're good for my spirits. I'm renting a car so I don't have to ruin your life every time I have to go somewhere."

"You're not ruining my life," I assured her.

"Even so. I think I know how to drive to your house."

"Six o'clock OK?"

"Perfect."

20

Ariana arrived with a small present for Eddie, a snow globe from the hotel's gift shop. Watching her give it to him, I thought, How could this lovely young woman have killed her parents? She was filled with kindness and warmth. She was thoughtful and considerate. The whole situation angered me.

After Eddie was in bed, the three of us sat around and talked. Ariana took her wallet out of her bag and removed some snapshots from a plastic sleeve. "I forgot I had this," she said, handing a photo to Jack, who was closer.

"Your parents' wedding picture," he said.

"Mom gave it to me. I don't remember when. If you look at the right side, you'll see where it's been trimmed."

He ran a finger over the edge. "Yeah, I see it. Either someone was standing next to your mother, or some other piece of identification was there." He passed it to me.

Once again the similarity between mother and daughter struck me. "How old was she when she married?" I asked.

"A little older than I am now. And Daddy was older than that. Mom had worked for a while."

"Doing what?"

"She may have taught. I'm not sure she was ever clear about it."

Once again a curtain veiled her mother's past. "Ariana, why did it take so long for you to come to Oakwood to look for your parents?"

"I—I was busy."

"Doing what?" Jack asked.

It was obvious she didn't want to say. "There was a guy in my life."

"And?" You don't get a gold shield accepting an answer like that.

"And we were, you know, engrossed in each other."

"For how long?"

"A couple of weeks."

"Can you give us his name, address, and phone number?"

"I can't."

We both sat looking at her, saying nothing.

"I can give you his name," she said. "But I don't know where he is. He took off for South America and I haven't heard from him since."

"What's in South America?" Jack persisted.

"It's an archeological dig in Guatemala. He's an interesting guy and I was really taken with him. I knew he was going away, but we, you know, got involved."

And time just passed, I thought, and she didn't think of her parents.

"Did he room with anyone?" I asked.

"He had a roommate, but not on a regular basis."

"Is he coming back to that apartment after the dig?"

She sighed. "I don't know. I don't know if he knows."

"Give us his name then, and his last address," Jack said.

She took a little notebook from her bag and wrote on a sheet of paper. She handed it to Jack, looking a little embarrassed.

"What day did he leave?" he asked.

She gave him an approximate date.

"Then you came here soon after," I said.

"I kind of came back to my senses after he left and I realized I hadn't heard from my parents for a while—since just before their anniversary. I started calling and they never answered. I got scared, especially because it was so long since the last time Mom had called."

"Do you mind if we check this out?" Jack asked.

She shook her head. "I'm innocent. Why should I mind?"

"Can we keep this picture of your parents?"

"I'd rather you didn't. It's my only copy. There's a camera store near the motel. I went inside and they have one of those instant picture machines. I'll make you a copy tomorrow."

I had used a machine like that once and I was impressed with the quality of the copy. "And a picture of yourself?" I said.

She was on her guard. "What for?"

"Just in case I need it."

"OK."

I looked at my watch. "I want to go over to the apartments and see if the man who saw your parents loading the SUV is at home."

"May I come, too?"

"Sure, if you want to."

"Then let's go."

I was pleased she had offered. It meant she wasn't afraid of being recognized by this man, probably because she hadn't been here. We took my car and drove over.

The name Joe had given me was George Benson. I found his entrance and we went up a flight of stairs. A woman opened the door. I made the introductions, reminding her of the disappearance and murder of the two tenants.

"The Mitchells, yes. I used to say hello to them. Come in."

The apartment was the same floor plan as the Brinkers'. We sat in the living room while Mrs. Benson went to fetch her husband.

"Mrs. Brooks, hello," he said, coming to join us. "I'm the one who saw the Mitchells loading their SUV. What can I do for you?"

"This is Ariana, the Mitchells' daughter."

"I'm sorry for your loss," Mr. Benson said soberly.

I took out the sketches and a recent snapshot of her parents Ariana had found in her wallet. "Are these the people you saw loading the SUV?"

He put his glasses on, sat on the sofa, and inspected the pictures. He nodded. "That's her. I'm sure of it. I can't be sure about the man. It was dark, remember, and I knew her a lot better than I knew him."

"How is that?"

"We often left for work around the same time in the morning, and I'd see her getting into the driver's seat. He was usually in the back. Sometimes he'd give me a wave, but I think he was more interested in the paper than in being social. Let's just say she was more outgoing."

"So you're only sure of the woman."

"I'd have to say so."

"Do you remember what you said to each other?"

"Hmm. Something light. We were neighbors, not friends. And I'm always on the move. I don't spend a lot of time making small talk. I must have come home late that night, and I was in a hurry to get upstairs and have some dinner. I probably said something about loading the furniture.

No. Wait. You know what? I saw they were having a tough time with whatever they were putting in the back and I asked if I could help. She said, 'That's all right. We're doing fine.' That's what we said. I remember it now."

"And what did you do?"

"I just continued on my way. I don't think I ever saw them again."

Mrs. Benson had nothing to add. She knew who they were too but had never said anything more than hello to them. She said that to everyone, she told me. She tried to be friendly.

We drove home. I returned the picture of Ariana's parents and she agreed to have a copy made of that, too. The photographic paper on which copies were made had ample room for several snapshots. When I pulled into the driveway, she said good night and got in her rental car. Tomorrow she would take the train into the city and talk to Arnold Gold. We would talk when she got back to the motel.

"I made some phone calls while you were gone," Jack said. He flicked off the television set as I sat down.

"To Chicago, I bet."

"No use waiting. This phone number Ariana gave us has been disconnected."

"This is the boyfriend who went to Guatemala?"

"And his sometime roommate. Well, they're both out of the apartment. There's a forwarding number somewhere in Michigan. I tried that. The guy exists. I talked to his mother. As far as she knows, he's in Guatemala."

"So Ariana really knew him."

"Looks like it, but Joe Fox could make a case that it was

someone she knew couldn't be contacted so she gave us this number."

"Jack, Joe Fox can make a case for any imaginary situation he chooses to cast doubt on. She gave us the name and number readily when you asked for it. And I can tell you the people we saw at the apartments definitely didn't recognize her. I'm going to figure this out, if only to get her off the hook."

"You sound angry."

"I've been fuming since Joe intimated Ariana was a suspect."

"So what's next?"

"Ariana's seeing Arnold tomorrow. She said she can get herself into the city and back. She'll call when she's back at the motel."

"And you?"

"Do you remember your son is graduating from kindergarten on Wednesday?"

"I sure as hell do. I'm taking the day off, remember."

"Good. And your folks are coming out."

"With a camera and tripod and video thing."

"Life has changed," I said.

"You bet it has."

21

I heard from Arnold before Ariana called. As circumspect as ever, he told me only that he was going to represent her and that if she was called to talk to anyone official about the deaths of her parents, she would do it only when he was present. He did not anticipate that she would ever be charged, which relieved me greatly. I had no idea how much she had told him, but I knew how to be as circumspect as he and I added nothing to what he already knew.

On Tuesday after lunch I called Jessie Brinker. She had nothing hard to report although she had made many phone calls.

"Jessie, can you access old local newspapers? They may be on microfilm in the library or at the newspaper building itself. And I guess it's possible they're on-line as well."

"What do you need?"

"A wedding announcement for Elaine Lysaught and Ronald Brinker. Maybe there's even an article written about them that would mention names."

"I'll look into it."

I gave her the date of the wedding and warned her that an announcement could appear in the issue of the day before or after, as well as on the date of the wedding. Maybe,

I said, there was mention of a maid of honor or even a list of ushers and bridesmaids, if it was a big enough wedding. Some of those people might still live in the area. I hoped.

I had intended to check the papers myself when we were in Portland, but we had rushed back to Madison after we heard the SUV was found there and I hadn't had the chance. Now I would have to rely on secondhand information, but Jessie seemed sharp and eager to help.

Ariana came over in late afternoon looking much better than when she had come out of Joe Fox's office yesterday. Her smile was back. Arnold was wonderful, she said. He believed in her and had warned her not to say a word to the police if she wasn't in his company.

"And here are the pictures," she said. "I had them made when I came back. You can cut them if you want. I can't tell them from the originals."

I couldn't either. I cut them carefully with my kitchen scissors. There were wide margins between them and I left them that way. I didn't want to lose even the tiniest scrap of information.

I told her about my conversation with Jessie.

"That's a great idea," she said. "You know, I bet there was an article when my folks got married. My father's parents were pretty important in the salmon industry. That's the kind of thing that gets some notice in the papers."

"You're right. Let's see if Jessie comes up with something."

We talked about Arnold over dinner and then, when Eddie seemed bored, we switched to his graduation. He had a new pair of summer pants and a short-sleeved shirt he could wear without a tie. He also had a new leather belt he had been saving for the event. Grandma and Grandpa were coming and would take us to lunch when the event was over. A graduation ceremony seemed more appropriate to eighth grade than kindergarten, but that's the way it is now.

Joe Fox called after dinner and said his investigators had located a U-Haul that had rented out a truck around the time I received the original phone call. A man came in, gave a cash deposit, and returned the truck several days later, paying cash. He couldn't be sure, of course, but it could have been the killers. Only about a hundred miles had been clocked.

"Did they respond to the sketches?" I asked.

"Unfortunately, the person who rented out the truck moved away, so there was no one there who would recognize it. Not that they'd remember one face so many weeks later."

Big deal, I thought. Someone rented a U-Haul for a few days and paid cash. "Any more furniture turn up?"

"We think a few pieces may have been dumped in an area where some homeless people congregate. Someone definitely dropped off a lot of clothes and they're gone. No surprise there. You talk to the guy in the apartments who saw them loading that SUV?"

"I did and I didn't learn anything. He couldn't even identify the man—said it was dark and he didn't know him well."

"About what we heard. Keep me in mind if anything new turns up."

I said, "Ditto," and hung up.

The big graduation day arrived, along with my in-laws. As Jack had predicted, they came with enough photographic equipment to cover a huge wedding. We all sat together and I watched as parent after parent jumped to his feet as a child took the stage to perform. When Eddie came on, both Jack and Grandpa Brooks leaped up and began filming. I felt vaguely embarrassed. Jack took several still shots and sat down, but my father-in-law stood during the entire rendition of "When Irish Eyes Are Smiling." Eddie had a sweet soprano voice, and we had picked this Irish tune for the benefit of the grandparents.

There were plenty of smiles and hugs when the ceremony was done. Every child came away with a certificate, and there were cookies and punch to enjoy. I was glad to have the opportunity to introduce Jack to the mothers I had met during the year. He had heard about them, as I heard about cops in his precinct or office, and I could see he was pleased to put faces to the names and stories.

When the festivities were over, we all went out for a fine lunch and then returned home. My cousin Gene was with us. He and Eddie are great buddies and my in-laws understand that Gene is a close part of the family. He was dressed more formally than we were and I persuaded him to take his jacket off in the restaurant and be comfortable. After my in-laws returned to Brooklyn, Gene stayed on and played with Eddie till late in the afternoon.

It was a satisfying day. When it was just the three of us again, I went to the phone to call Ariana, but before I picked it up, it rang.

"Where's the girl?"

It took me a second to fit the angry voice to Joe Fox.

"Excuse me?"

"Mrs. Brooks, this is Joe Fox. Where is Ariana Brinker?"

"I don't know. I haven't seen her today. We had a family affair. I was just about to call her at the hotel."

"Don't bother. She's gone."

"What do you mean?"

"She checked out of the hotel."

I looked down at the answering machine to see if it was blinking, but it wasn't. "I'm sorry. I don't understand. I haven't seen her and she hasn't left a message."

"She's skedaddled, Mrs. Brooks. You'll never see her again. She knows we were closing in on her and she's taken off. Do you know if she has a passport?"

"I have no idea."

"I expect she's out of the country by now."

"I don't think so," I said, thinking that she would not leave without her stash. She would have to return to Chicago first—if she had told me the truth about where she put the money.

"Why not?"

"Because she has an estate lawyer in New York and I'm sure she's heir to whatever her parents left behind. And she was determined to bury her parents. That was very important to her."

"She's a good actress, that one," he said gruffly. "She says what she wants you to hear. Who's her estate lawyer?"

I didn't want to tell him. The truth was, I had forgotten her name although I could see her clearly in my mind. "I don't know. She's in New York. That's all I remember."

"What's the girl's Chicago address?"

"I have no idea. She said she had traded apartments with a friend—and I don't know the friend's name and don't know what her previous address was."

"For a woman with a lot of information, you're missing some fundamental items."

His tone and insinuations annoyed me. "I've told you what I know. There isn't any more."

"Stay in touch." He hung up.

Before telling Jack what had happened, I called the motel and asked for Ariana Brinker.

A second voice came on and asked who I was.

"Christine Bennett Brooks."

"Mrs. Brooks, Ms. Brinker left a message for you in case you called. Just a minute, please." She put me on hold briefly. "Here it is. 'I'm OK. Don't worry about me. You'll hear from me.' "

I hung up the phone and told Jack.

"I don't like it," he said. "My gut tells me something's wrong."

Mine did too but I tried to ignore it. "She wouldn't leave the country without the money."

"Maybe she put it into checking accounts instead of safe-deposit boxes."

I hadn't thought of that. "How many checking accounts could she open?"

"As many as she had time for. She might have gotten certificates of deposit. When they came due, she could transfer them easily into checking accounts or have the bank send her a check, wherever she was."

"She didn't run," I said.

"Boy, you get stubborn when you defend someone you like."

"So do you. It's not such a bad trait. She's innocent, Jack. She didn't murder her parents."

"Have it your way."

I didn't respond.

I sat for several minutes, thinking. Finally, I called the motel back. "Did Miss Brinker take a shuttle to one of the airports or order a taxi?" I asked the young man who answered.

"I wasn't on duty," he said. "Can I call you back when I've checked?"

"Please." I gave him my number and sat down to wait.

Five minutes later he reported back. "I've checked the shuttle lists and she's not on it. And I called the taxi company we use and they didn't pick her up."

"Thanks so much. I appreciate your looking into this."

She must have taken the rental car to one of the airports, I thought. I didn't know what company she had used or if she had gotten it through the hotel. Why did you do this, Ariana? I thought. You must have known how bad it would look.

The phone rang, jarring me. I had put it on the table next to my chair. I grabbed it and answered. There was a lot of noise at the far end.

"Chris? It's me, Ariana."

"Ariana, thank goodness." I saw Jack look up.

"Did you get my message?"

"Yes, but I'm worried anyway. And Detective Fox called. He's furious."

"I don't care about him. I care about you. I just wanted you to know I'm all right and you shouldn't worry."

"Where are you?"

"In an airport."

"I can tell that. Which airport? Let me come and get you."

"No. Listen, I've got a pile of quarters here and I'm afraid they'll run out before I tell you something very important."

"I'm listening."

"I know who did it, who killed my parents. I don't know if I can prove it, but I'm going to try."

"What are you talking about?" I said.

"I think I know the motive. Listen to me, I sound like a cop, don't I?"

"You really know who did it?"

"I think so. I figured it out. I want a little more information and I think I know where to find it."

"You're not leaving the country."

"Why would I do that?"

"Detective Fox thinks that's where you've gone."

The operator came on and I waited while she deposited a few dollars' worth of quarters.

Then she said, "Are you still there, Chris?"

"I'm here, yes. Tell me what you know."

"Not yet. It sounds so crazy. I think they did it for the money."

"Was the money originally stolen?"

"I don't think so. I think my parents got it from my grandmother just as they told me. At least, it's possible."

"Can I join you wherever you are?"

"You've done enough. Stay home with your family. I'll let you know what I find."

"Ariana, Jack and I are—"

"I have to go," she said, interrupting. "Good-bye." She hung up before I could respond.

Jack listened patiently as I related every word I could remember of the conversation. "And she wouldn't tell you where she is or where she's going?"

"No. She's in an airport, but it doesn't have to be one of the New York ones. I suspect she hopped on a flight this afternoon and she's on the second leg to wherever she's going."

"She didn't give you any clue who the killer is or how she figured it out?"

"Nothing, but she did say it was about the money."

"But you don't know why she thinks that."

I shook my head. "Joseph said it only looked like it was about the money, but that it wasn't, that it was about something much more important."

"Remember that Sister Joseph sees a lot of things differently from the way other people do."

"I know." I was racking my brain to figure out what it was that might have tipped her off.

"Chris, you have every piece of information that Ariana has. You gave her most of what she knows. You've been to every place she's gone to. If she can figure it out, so can you."

"She must have sat in the hotel room last night or this morning and thought about it. She had the letters from the two lawyers, both written by her parents. Maybe they said something that she didn't read to me. Maybe they tried to give her some hint."

"I don't think so," Jack said. "They spent their lives keeping information from her. Why would they turn around and tell her what they had worked so hard to keep secret? And why a hint? If they wanted her to know, they'd tell her outright. I don't think it's in those letters."

"Then what?" What? I asked myself again. What? There was the folder of papers I had seen in the desk that had been found abandoned in a field. Except for the newspaper clipping describing my exploits here in town last year, there had been nothing of interest. There were the pictures she had copied for me. What else? The money, the SUV, the empty apartment. Maybe a U-Haul had been rented, but so what? It had been returned and used a dozen times. We had spoken to Mr. Benson Monday night, the man who had seen the Brinkers load their SUV with furniture.

Why had they loaded their SUV if they weren't moving anywhere?

"You look like you're burning up a lot of brain cells."

"Why did they load the SUV if they weren't moving anywhere?"

"Good question. Maybe they were moving and these people finished the job for them. Maybe they helped the killers at gunpoint."

"Yes," I said. "And maybe something else."

22

I sat by myself trying to think where Ariana was headed. There were three possible destinations, unless she knew something I could not imagine. The first was Madison. The money had been there and the house was there. For a while, at least, the killers had been there. If she were lying about having figured it out and wanted only a little time to settle her affairs, take the money, and run, then she could be on her way to Chicago. But suppose she had lied about putting the money away in Chicago. I had left her in Madison. She could have deposited the money in banks in Wisconsin, or even in banks along her drive from Madison to Chicago. If the money wasn't all in one city, it would be hard to find. I didn't even want to think about that, but it sounded like a reasonable thing to do, and not difficult.

It was even possible that she had reburied the money behind the house, although I thought that would be dangerous. The killers had been to Madison, might even still be there, and might decide to dig up the yard at their leisure. No one was living in the house, the window had been repaired, and the neighbors couldn't see over the shrubbery. What had given us privacy might allow them to do damage without being seen.

The third destination was Portland. What could she hope to find there? I had asked Jessie Brinker to check some things for me and I hadn't heard from her, but that wasn't surprising. I had just talked to her yesterday.

If Ariana had flown to Madison, she would have had to change planes and could have called from the airport in Chicago or Detroit between flights. Both Chicago and Portland were likely to be direct flights.

I went to my notes and found the list of phone numbers she had given me. I had one for Wally Keller at his office and another at his home. I reached for the phone and dialed the home number.

His wife answered and called him to pick up.

"Mrs. Brooks?" he said.

"Yes. I hope I'm not intruding. Have you heard from Ariana today?"

"Haven't heard a word since the three of us looked at the things in that SUV. Is something wrong?"

"I'm just trying to chase her down," I said lightly. "She was here for a while. I thought she might be on her way to Madison."

"She could be, but she didn't tell me. Any developments on the homicides?"

"Not so far. I don't suppose the Madison police arrested the driver of that SUV?"

"Nah. I've talked to them a couple of times. I think those folks came back, found the car towed, and high-tailed it out of town."

"You're probably right. Mr. Keller, if Ariana turns up, would you give me a ring?" I said it casually.

"Tell you what. If she comes here, I'll tell her you called."

"That's fine." Lawyers, I thought. I hadn't been clever

enough. He wasn't going to tattle on Ariana, who was his client. If she wanted me to know she was there, she would call. I wasn't getting anything out of him.

Before we finished the conversation, he told me the SUV and its contents were being shipped to New York State and should arrive any day. The Madison police had no reason to hold it any longer.

I had a feeling that if Ariana had told him she was coming but hadn't cautioned him that the trip was a secret, I might have caught him off guard when I asked if he had heard from her. I was pretty sure she hadn't called him. Which didn't answer any questions definitively for me. She could still be on her way there. Or to the other two destinations.

Chicago had only the money, if it was there, and her apartment. It wasn't involved in the homicides. But wherever she was going, I couldn't get out of my mind the fact that she wanted to bury her parents. I didn't think it was an act. I was sure she cared.

"Jack," I said, trying to think what to do next, "do you have that phone number for the parents of the guy in Guatemala?"

"Yeah, it should be here." He messed around some papers on the coffee table, which looked as though a tornado had hit it. I'd better get back to tidying up, I thought. "Here." He handed me the slip of paper on which Ariana had written the boyfriend's name, Barry Tedesco, and his apartment phone number. Jack had added the forwarding number in big black numerals.

I called the number and a woman answered.

"Mrs. Tedesco?"

"Yes."

"I'm Chris Bennett Brooks. You talked to my husband last night about your son in Guatemala."

"Oh yes. Is something wrong?"

"Not at all. I wondered if there was any way I could reach your son by phone."

"That's not too easy. Sometimes they're miles from the place where there's a telephone line. But you can leave a message and he might be able to get back to you at some point. He's called me once since he got down there. And they've got a computer where the phone is. Do you have an e-mail address?"

I found myself smiling, happy Jack had convinced me to get on-line. "Yes, I do." I gave her my address and she gave me her son's and the phone number. "Did he ever mention Ariana to you, Mrs. Tedesco?"

"He said he'd met a very nice girl and I was really pleased. Sometimes my husband and I think he works too hard and should play a little. Is there a problem?" She sounded a bit apprehensive.

"Nothing to worry about. She's had some bad luck and I think your son may be able to help with some information."

"I see." She said it as though she didn't.

"Thank you very much. I'll e-mail him and maybe leave a phone message."

I'm sure I left her wondering, but I didn't think a long story would help either of us.

I had never called overseas before, but it was straightforward. After keying several numbers, I heard a ring. Almost immediately someone answered, speaking Spanish.

Ouch, I thought. I speak some French and I know some Latin, but Spanish is beyond me. "Hello?" I said. "Do you speak English?"

"Oh, sure," a man's voice said. "Better than Spanish."

"Oh, good. I'm looking for Barry Tedesco."

"Barry, yeah. He's out at the dig but I think he's coming back tomorrow. Want to leave a message?"

I asked to have Barry call me or e-mail me. I explained I was a friend of Ariana Brinker, her parents had been involved in an accident, and I needed some information from him. The man I was talking to said he hoped it wasn't serious and promised that Barry would get the message the minute he walked into the office. Upstairs, I typed an e-mail message saying substantially the same thing and sent it off. Now I would have to wait.

A little while later, I got a surprising phone call. It was George Benson, whom we'd visited Monday night.

"Mrs. Brooks," he said, "I thought of something. It's probably not going to help you much, but I noticed something odd that night."

"I'm listening."

"The Mitchells who were loading their SUV? They were both wearing gloves."

"Really? On a warm night? What kind of gloves, did you notice?"

"The kind you wear around the garden—cotton, burlap, like that."

"Thank you very much," I said. "That's very interesting."

The Brinkers were wearing gloves. The Brinkers were loading their SUV so they could dump their possessions in a field or where homeless people congregate. Where was this going to end?

I did what I do when I can't think what else to do: I went over everything I had once again. I thought about Grandma Adelaide Brinker giving her son and daughter-in-law a

million dollars in used bills. Had she met them somewhere and handed over the suitcase? She must have known
that her son was being hunted. She never came to visit;
she was merely a voice on the phone to young Ariana.

"I'm going to bed," I said.

"Just like that?"

"I'm working myself into a headache. I don't want to
think about this case any more today."

"Let's go."

I got a call from Guatemala at eleven the next morning.

"This is Barry Tedesco. You called me?"

"Yes. Thanks so much for getting back to me."

"Is Ariana OK?"

"She's fine. There's nothing to worry about. Barry, after
you left for Guatemala, she found out something awful
had happened to her parents."

"She said she was worried. She hadn't called them for a
while."

"That's what my question is. Were you, uh, seeing her
before you left?"

"Seeing her? Yeah. I was seeing her. Why?"

"Because it seemed out of character that she didn't call
her parents for quite a while."

"She was with me. She worked during the day and I was
getting ready for this trip. I had a lot of things to do. But I
saw her every night. We were together a lot."

"For how long?"

"Two weeks, maybe more. I'm not sure. It was—uh—it
was pretty intense."

"Thanks, Barry."

"That's it? That's all you wanted to know?"

"Yes. Thanks for calling."

"How is she?"

"She's fine. Don't be concerned about her."

"Tell her I'll call her when I get back."

"I'll do that."

I felt real relief when I got off the phone. I was sure he was telling the truth. Evening was the only time Ariana could call her parents and that's when she was "intensely" occupied with Barry. I was sure she had nothing to do with the murders.

I called Jack and told him about the conversation with Barry Tedesco. He was impressed that Barry had called back so soon, but I thought it was just a lucky coincidence. Probably he had made the trip to pick up provisions and mail, maybe to report to someone. While we were talking, Jack told me he'd heard from Joe Fox. The Brinkers' SUV had arrived and was being carefully examined, along with its contents. A cursory once-over had not turned up anything important. And, oh yes, there seemed to be no prints on the vehicle that belonged to anyone besides the Brinkers. That he had learned from the Madison police.

"Mommy?"

"Yes, honey." I got up and went to the back door. Eddie had been playing out back, presumably picking weeds out of my garden, and hopefully not pulling up any of my fledgling tomato and pepper plants.

"Come and look," he said when I stepped outside. "There are flowers."

We walked back to the garden and he pointed. There were several yellow blossoms on the tomato plants. "Oh, how wonderful," I said. "You must be very careful not to touch the flowers. In a few days, you'll see tiny green tomatoes inside them."

"Why are they green?"

"Because they're not ripe. When they're red, we can pick them, but not before. Remember last summer?"

"Uh-huh."

"We waited till they were nice and ripe and then we went out every day and picked them. How's your weeding coming along?"

"I pulled out all those weeds." He pointed to a small pile and I walked over to inspect them. Sure enough, they were weeds.

"You're doing a great job. Now let's clean up the squash." I had planted them in hills, and the zucchini vines were really crawling. "These will have great big yellow flowers soon and the little squash will come after them."

Dropping to his knees, he started pulling small weeds that cluttered the path between the rows.

"I'll call you for lunch in a little while."

"OK."

I watched him for a minute before going back inside. It was time to put together lunch. And then I would think some more.

23

Breakthroughs come in different ways and at different times. I sensed on that Thursday that I had mined every source I could think of. I had Joseph's opinion, which I value greatly, and Jack and I had discussed this case often. I had satisfied myself, if not Jack, that Ariana was not the killer of her parents. First, she wasn't in Oakwood at the time. But more important, her parents had obviously been on the run ever since she was a child, and she certainly hadn't been a threat to them then. I also believed her when she said she had figured it out, even if I wasn't sure where she was right now.

After lunch I dropped Eddie off at a friend's house, thinking I should reciprocate and promising myself I would, as soon as I had this case solved. Back home I sat down at the dining room table once again, determined to see what Ariana had seen and that still eluded me.

Red checks in my notebook marked some of the facts that concerned me, including the most recent, that the Brinkers had been wearing gloves as they loaded the SUV. I was still troubled that Mrs. Brinker's driver's license was missing, but her husband's wasn't. And Joseph's feeling that this whole case was actually about something far more important than money rankled.

I was deep in thinking again when the phone rang.

"Chris? Hi, it's Jessie."

"Jessie, good to hear from you. Do you have anything for me?"

"I wish I did. I checked out two big newspapers for that date you gave me and also a couple of days before and after, and there's just nothing about the Brinker wedding."

"I'm so disappointed," I said. "I was so sure."

"It does seem strange, but I can tell you, I read every society page listing I could find. There was just nothing. Are you sure you have the right date?"

"Positive. Ariana knows exactly when her parents were married." I didn't mention that I had another source, too—that disturbing phone call.

"Well, I'm really sorry it didn't work out. If there's anything else you'd like me to check . . ." She left it hanging.

"No. Thanks so much for spending the time."

When I hung up, I acknowledged my disappointment. How could a wedding like that, a formal wedding with the groom a member of a prominent family, not have a notice? I guessed they wanted their privacy or had some other reason for not notifying the papers. It was a blow. I would have to work with what I had and that hadn't led me far enough at this point.

As I went back to the dining room, I took off the shelf a little brass turtle with a magnifier for its back. It stood just the right distance from the page to magnify an image. I laid the photograph of the Brinkers as bride and groom on the table in front of me and set the turtle on top of the right side of the picture, along the line where it had been trimmed. Everything was white, the bride's dress flowing down to the floor. Leaning over the magnifier, I moved it slowly down the cut edge of the picture. I had left a margin of half an inch but even so, the white of the photo was different from the white of the margin.

And then I saw it. There weren't two whites; there were three. One was Elaine Brinker's wedding dress, one was the white margin of the photo paper, and one was a tiny fold of another white dress. Either a white-gowned bridesmaid stood next to her—and I doubted that; the fabric was as long and flowing as Elaine Brinker's—or there had been a double wedding.

A double wedding, I thought, facts and images crowding my mind, almost making me dizzy. Who has a double wedding? Sisters. Sisters have double weddings. The Lysaught sisters had been married together. And then it hit me. Twins have double weddings. The Lysaught sisters were twins.

All the unexplained facts fell into place. I felt momentarily so overwhelmed I could not think which fact to consider first. Mr. Benson's call last night about the Brinkers wearing gloves. That's because they weren't the Brinkers. The woman was Elaine's twin sister. She had her own fingerprints. The man wasn't Ronald. He was probably the twin's husband. The missing driver's license. The twin could carry her sister's license and show it if a cop stopped her for an infraction. But her companion, whatever his name might be, couldn't carry Ronald Brinker's; it had a different picture on it. "This is my silver wedding anniversary." I had spoken to the twin, who was telling me the truth.

I looked again at the minuscule scrap of fabric that came from the second dress. Ariana had looked up the marriage license of her parents, using the name Brinker. Had she looked for the marriage of a woman named Lysaught, she would have found two; I was sure of it. And that's what she was doing right now. Sometime later today

I would get a triumphant call: I found it! My mother was a twin. Aunt Junie got it wrong. I didn't have a twin, my mother did.

Something had happened between the two sisters, something so enormous that Elaine's sister had set out to kill her. It had to be the money. Perhaps the twin's economic status had deteriorated and she asked for help, knowing through the family grapevine that Elaine had inherited a huge amount of money. But Elaine had not accommodated her sister, and what had been a very special and intense love had turned into hate.

Maybe at the beginning the twin wanted only to confront Elaine, but when days and months turned into years and the hatred became inflamed, the desire to confront turned into a desire to kill.

Even threatened with their lives, the Brinkers refused to disclose the location of the money. After the murder, the twin must have known that Ariana, unable to reach her parents, would try to find them. All the twin had to do was wait around inconspicuously and follow Ariana to the money. I could think of a dozen ways she could have done it.

I called Jack and told him. He let out a whistle of approval and surprise. "Nice going," he said. "A double wedding with twins. And you're right. Something happened between them and the twin wanted money that she didn't get. Wow!"

I smiled. Then I told him about Jessie's call and my hunch that Ariana was in Portland, not Madison, looking up information on her newfound aunt.

"She should watch her back," Jack said. "That's a dangerous woman out there, a multiple killer. She didn't find the money when she went to Madison and she wants it. She's got to grab Ariana."

"I don't know how to reach her except to call the hotel we both stayed in and if she's not there, just to phone other hotels. That's not going to be easy."

"Try that one for starters. Keep me posted."

I didn't have the bill for the hotel, as Ariana had paid for it, but I was pretty sure which one it was and what street it was on. The phone company came through with a number, and in another minute I confirmed that Ariana was there. They rang her room and I got her voice mail.

"Ariana, this is Chris. Here's my number." I rattled it off. "I must speak to you. It's urgent. I know what you've discovered. I looked at the wedding picture myself. Jack says you have to be very careful. She may still be watching you."

I hung up and called Joseph, repeating to her what I had told Jack.

"Very good," she said. "I think you're right. And I think the money is part of it. Is Ariana with you?"

"No. She left without saying where she was going. I tracked her down to Portland. I think she's checking records again, trying to find out this woman's married name."

"I expect this woman may be close to deranged after so many years of hunting down her sister, not to mention murdering her. Ariana should be careful."

I told her about the message I'd left.

"Keep after her, Chris. I don't like to think that anything could happen to her. She's not at fault for any of this."

"I know."

"One more thing: count the years. I think that's important."

She had to go then; she had someone in her office whom she had to get back to. I hung up thinking about her last instruction. I didn't know what years she was talking about. I would take a swim and hopefully it would come to me.

I picked up Eddie on my way home. This had been an amazing day, I thought. A call from Guatemala in the morning and a call to Portland in the afternoon. Talk about being cosmopolitan.

"Can I swim with you tomorrow?" Eddie asked as we reached our house.

"Sure. I didn't take you today because you were busy."

"I won't be busy tomorrow."

"OK, honey. You know, when your day camp starts, you'll swim there every day. Won't that be nice?"

"Uh-huh."

There was a message from Ariana, and I was relieved to hear her voice. "I knew you'd catch on, Chris. You should see what I dug up. Call me when you get home."

I did that. "Ariana," I began, "Jack thinks you may be in danger. She may be following you."

"I don't think she followed me here. She lost my trail in Madison."

"Let's hope so, but we can't be sure. I think you should get on the next plane to New York. Call me from the airport so I know when you're arriving. You can stay here if you want."

"OK. I should have enough information now. This aunt of mine married a man named Stuart Trent. Her name is Eileen. Elaine and Eileen. Cute, huh? How could my grandparents have done that?"

"It was probably the style at the time."

"Anyway, what a wedding that was. Unbelievable. Listen, I looked up Stuart Trent, and he's not in the phone book. Neither is Eileen Trent. I called information and they're not in Portland."

"Ariana, you're making me very nervous. Please don't even try to call them. They murdered your parents. If they're after the money, you could be next."

"I know. You're right. OK, I'll pack my bag and head for the airport."

I gave the whole thing some thought. If this twin had a vendetta against Elaine and Ronald Brinker, maybe it had destroyed her marriage. I called Arnold Gold and told him what we had learned.

"You're fantastic," he said, "not that I ever thought otherwise."

"This was a joint operation, Arnold. Here's my problem. I think there's a good chance this woman, Eileen Lysaught Trent, is divorced. Is there a way to find out? Do you by any chance have a trusted old friend practicing law in Portland?"

"As a matter of fact, I do. Harriet and I went out to the West Coast a couple of years ago and visited him and his wife. He can find out if this woman is divorced, but it may take some time."

"Oh." I'm sure my disappointment was audible.

"But who knows? We may get lucky. I'll get back to you."

He called back in less than half an hour. "Looks like we're in luck. He's got a private investigator that he says is the best in the business. This fellow specializes in divorce work and he'll know who to seek out in the records department. That's the best I can do for you."

"Arnold, it's more than I could ask for. We've got to find

this aunt of Ariana's before she finds Ariana. I don't want to think what might happen."

"Agreed. So why didn't she hit Ariana in Oakwood?"

"She didn't have the chance. Ariana arrived at night and went to her parents' apartment. This aunt couldn't spend twenty-four hours a day watching the door. The next morning, when Ariana arrived again at the apartment complex, she went straight from the taxi to the building manager's office. Ariana stayed there till I arrived and I took her to our house."

"I see."

"And from there the aunt essentially followed us to Madison. She probably saw what airline we went to and either found out from the baggage guy where we were going or called the airline and pretended to be Ariana. Then she got in the SUV and drove out to Madison."

"Lot of driving."

"But doable."

"OK. You'll hear from me as soon as I have something to tell you."

When I was setting the table for dinner, Ariana called from the Portland airport. She was standby on a flight east; if she didn't make it, she would try for another. Not to worry. She would call when she arrived at the hotel.

It was Friday morning when she eventually called, sounding half asleep. She had had a long layover somewhere along the way, but she was safe and sound at the hotel, the DO NOT DISTURB sign was on the door, and she expected to sleep for the next several hours. She would call when her day began.

Ariana called about noon, and when I went to pick her up, I took special care when I left the house to see if a car was parked along the street or an unfamiliar woman was strolling in the neighborhood. Observing nothing unusual, I sensed that Ariana was right; the aunt had lost her trail in Madison.

Ariana, Eddie, and I went out for lunch. Eddie thought that was just great. He was so involved in eating his sloppy cheeseburger, he had little to say. Ariana and I made up for it.

Starting with my discovery of the second wedding dress in the picture, I went through everything, including the call to Guatemala, which surprised her and put a smile on her face. I finished with my call to Arnold.

"A divorce. I never thought of that," she said. "But you're right. A woman like that must be hard to live with."

"We may not hear for a while, but Arnold said his lawyer friend had a very good investigator who would work on it. I suspect more changes hands than pieces of paper."

"I see. And once we know what name she's using right now, we should notify the police."

"We can tell Joe Fox, if he's still speaking to me. He wasn't very happy when you left town."

"I couldn't sit around and wait while nothing was happening. I had to make something happen."

"And you did."

"So now we know who's been hounding my parents all these years and why they were doing it."

"And if we're right, they could still be after you." I glanced over at Eddie, unwilling to have him hear what awful things went on in the world around him, but he was working on his dripping burger with great dedication.

"What do we do now?"

"We hope to hear from Arnold soon and then we take what we have to Detective Fox. When they pick up this woman, she's likely to have your mother's driver's license and other things that clearly came from, you know." I glanced at Eddie.

"Chris, what we found in Madison, that's still between us. OK?"

"Fine."

"I still don't know for sure where it came from, but I believe it was an inheritance."

"So do I."

"That was good," Eddie said. He turned his face toward me and I almost laughed. Ketchup, relish, and assorted other drippings encircled his mouth. He stuck his tongue out to get the last of it before I applied a thick paper napkin to his face.

Ariana laughed. "I'm not a good influence," she said. "I'm always on the kid's side."

24

The call from Arnold came after we'd had dinner. His lawyer friend had called him at home. The detective had done his job and done it well. He knew this one and that one, and he could get a favor when he needed it.

"I have news for you," Arnold said. "This woman, this Eileen Lysaught Trent, wasn't Mrs. Trent for very long. The date of her first marriage is the one you gave me, but she divorced less than two years later."

"Two years?" I said.

"That's what the court papers say. Then she remarried, let's see, about five years later. The new husband's name was Owen Foster. She divorced him eight years after that."

"Busy lady. Do we know for certain that that's her name? Foster?"

"It's the name she goes by."

"So she's single now. That means it wasn't her husband who helped her hunt down the Brinkers."

"Apparently not. The investigator did some more digging and found her address and where she works. She's a part-time nurse at a local Portland hospital."

"A nurse," I breathed. "She might have access to chloroform."

"Might indeed. Looks like you've done it, Chris. You planning to share this information with the authorities?"

"Yes, but not tonight. I can't thank you and your friend in Portland enough."

"Can't live without friends. Remember me to Jack."

Ariana had gone upstairs to put Eddie to bed, taking her lovely bag with her. She said she had a small present for him. When she came downstairs, I told her and Jack what Arnold had said.

"Then we know where she is," Ariana said excitedly. "They can arrest her."

"I'm sure they will," Jack said. "Assuming she's there. This gal does a lot of running around."

"What an awful life she's lived," I said. "Two husbands, two divorces. Arnold said the first divorce was less than two years after the wedding."

"And you can bet it was gathering steam for a long time before it got to court. It must have been a disaster from the beginning."

"So she needed money and her sister wouldn't give her any."

"Her sister didn't have to," Ariana said with irritation. "My father's mother bequeathed that money to her son, not to her daughter-in-law's sister."

"You're right. I'm just looking at it from your aunt's point of view."

"How did she even know about it?"

"It must have been in all the papers when your grandfather died. They probably referred to him as a millionaire businessman. I notice they do that all the time now. Fifteen years ago a million dollars was a lot of money."

"Fifteen years ago," Ariana said.

"Isn't that when you lived in Madison and talked to your grandmother over the phone?"

She nodded, but I could see something was bothering her.

Something was bothering me, too. I didn't say anything at that moment, because things were still a bit fuzzy. Before I ran Ariana back to the motel, we all talked for a while, had coffee and cookies. Tomorrow, we decided, we would get in touch with Joe Fox and tell him what we had learned. Or perhaps, Ariana suggested politely, I would do it, without telling him she was here in town. She didn't look forward to being hauled down to his interrogation room.

And then she said, somewhat tentatively, "What did Barry say when you talked to him?"

It took me a couple of seconds to recall whom the name belonged to. It was her Chicago boyfriend, now archeologist in Guatemala.

"He was very concerned about you," I said. "I think he really cares."

"Good." She took a deep breath. "Because I do, too."

Jack fell asleep quickly but I didn't. What was bothering me? We had learned so much in the last day or two; we knew the identity of the killer and where to find her. What was still gnawing at me?

Count the years, Joseph had said. What years? What was I forgetting? I didn't know the exact time that Ronald's father had died, but the money must have been given to Ronald about fifteen years ago, give or take a year or two. The Brinkers were then living in Madison. What was wrong with that?

Think, Kix, I ordered myself. Adelaide gave the money to Ronald Brinker during her lifetime to make certain he would get what was his due and she left nothing to him in her will. That was fine. They got together somewhere, she handed over the money, they kissed good-bye, and he went back to Madison. What was wrong with that?

I turned my back against Jack's chest. How nice it was to be married to a warm, comfortable man. His arm moved to cover me and I wriggled closer. Something I hadn't seen, something Joseph had observed. I was too close to this now. What wasn't I seeing?

Count the years. What years? Twenty-five? Ariana's age? And then I saw it. I sat up in bed like a shot, dislodging Jack's arm and pulling the summer blanket off him.

"Huh?" He put his hand on my back. "You OK, honey?"

"Jack, she wasn't their child."

"What? What are you talking about?"

"Ariana. She wasn't the Brinkers' child."

"What do you mean?"

"Joseph was right. This wasn't about money. The money came later, when Ariana was five or six or seven years old. The Brinkers moved out of Portland when she was a baby. She's the twin's daughter."

"Jeez." He sat himself up beside me. "You want to run that by me again?"

"The twin was pregnant. But by the time the baby was about to be born, or maybe even sooner, she'd broken up with her husband. She talked to Elaine and Elaine said she would take the child. The twin gave her name as Elaine Brinker in the hospital. She gave birth to Ariana and handed the baby over to Elaine."

"OK so far."

I turned to look at him in the light that came through the shades. "And then she changed her mind."

"And wanted the baby back."

"Right. And they couldn't do that. She was their child by then. They loved her. So they picked up and ran."

"Wow."

"It fits," I said. "Joseph was right. It wasn't about money. It was something much more profound, much more important. It was about keeping their child. The money came later. They didn't need it so they saved it for Ariana by burying it."

"So at first the twin chased them to get the baby back and then, when she kept losing them, she hunted them down to kill them for keeping her child."

"That's it. That's what happened."

"So what happened to the first husband, the father of the child?"

"Who knows? It doesn't even matter. Maybe he was a disaster as a human being, didn't care about the baby or about his wife. He just wanted out. But she kept on."

"I think you've got it," he said. "This is certainly a stronger motive for murder than money is, even a lot of money. And I see now why Elaine would have to cut off all ties to her natural family. Her mother probably knew what was going on and might turn her in to be fair to the twin."

"Yes," I said, nodding. "They could stay in touch with the Brinkers quietly, surreptitiously, but not with the Lysaughts. Elaine couldn't trust her own mother on this. Jack, what an awful situation, fighting over a baby."

"And who would guess? Ariana looked like her mother, which meant she looked like her adoptive mother. It was just perfect. So who did this Eileen enlist to help her kill the Brinkers?"

I shrugged. "What difference does it make? Maybe a boyfriend, maybe a hired detective."

"Not if he's licensed. That's the end of his career at the very least if she gives him up."

"I have to call Arnold. I want that Portland detective to do a little more digging. Just to fill in the blanks, I'd like to know when the Brinker grandfather died, which would be the time he left money to his wife and maybe his children, and when Grandma Adelaide died."

Jack glanced at the lighted clock on his night table. "Not now, Chris. You may be wide awake, but the rest of the world isn't."

"I have to tell her, don't I?"

"Ariana? If you don't, it'll come out. That'll be Aunt Eileen's defense, that her child was stolen and it ruined her life."

"Can she prove it? The birth certificate lists Elaine and Ronald Brinker as parents."

"Don't forget DNA."

"Right. Even if the twins' DNA is similar, Ronald will be ruled out as the father."

"This is really something. You put the whole damn thing together."

"Oh my. But will I sleep?"

Jack pulled me down. "Let's give it a try, huh?"

Saturday is not the time to accomplish business but I wanted Arnold to talk to his Portland lawyer friend so the detective could get to work early Monday.

"That's some theory," Arnold said on the phone, a familiar piano sonata playing in the background.

"I think it's right. Here's what I'd like to know: When did Grandfather Brinker die? That should be in the local papers. And when did his wife, Adelaide, die? I don't recall his first name but it'll be in her obituary."

"What's that going to tell you?"

"When the money passed from Grandpa to Grandma. I think she must have arranged to hand over during her lifetime however much was destined for Ronald because she knew he couldn't come out of hiding to claim it after her death."

"Why do you need to know that?"

"I want a chronology. If the Brinkers left Portland before the grandfather died, it must have been because of the baby, not because of money."

"You have any idea how much money was involved?"

I realized Arnold didn't know about the money buried in Madison. "No. Ariana hasn't claimed her inheritance yet. When she gets the death certificate, she'll take care of that."

"OK. I'll call and pass along your questions."

The next thing I had to do was harder. I called Ariana and said we should get together. I picked her up at the motel and drove over to the cove that our family and many others in the area own in common, a semicircle of sandy beach on the Long Island Sound. This is my favorite place in Oakwood. When I first moved into Aunt Meg's house, I used to walk here to think, to get close to the things I loved—the water, the sand, the wind.

"Where are we?" Ariana asked.

"A private beach that a group of families in Oakwood owns. Feel like a walk?"

She looked at me with apprehension. "What's going on?"

"I have something to tell you and I don't want an inquisitive five-year-old around."

She opened the door of the car, took her shoes off, as I did, and we started walking. As usual, there were few people on the beach. It was difficult to swim here—waves battered the shore—but it was a refreshing stroll. An old woman sat on her aluminum chair, an umbrella protecting her from the sun's rays. I waved as we passed her, not sure who she was, but she was a neighbor.

"I figured something out last night, Ariana. It explains a lot of things but it will surely bring turmoil to your life."

"Maybe I don't need to hear it."

We walked and I said nothing.

"OK, do it. Tell me. I can't stand this."

"Your mother's twin is your natural mother."

She stopped and looked at me, her eyes large and dark, peering into my thoughts. Then she whispered, "No."

"It's why your parents left Portland when you were a baby."

Two tears ran down her cheeks. "It wasn't the money? I thought you said it was the money."

"My feeling is that your grandfather didn't die when you were a baby. The money wasn't distributed until years later."

"I can't believe this."

We resumed walking. It was morning and the sand was still a comfortable temperature. Later today, it might be so hot you would need to cover your feet for protection.

"I see," she said, her voice unsteady. "It explains a few things, doesn't it?"

"Several." I ran through them: why the people putting furniture into the SUV were wearing gloves, why Elaine's driver's license was missing but her husband's wasn't, perhaps why the blood found in the apartment belonged to neither victim.

"This is—this is hard to accept."

"I know."

"Was she going to kill me, too?"

"I don't know. I'd like to think not. Originally, she probably just wanted you back. As time went on, she must have realized that couldn't be. She became angry, enraged. Eventually, she wanted to kill, but I don't think she wanted to hurt you. I think she felt love for you."

"How can this have happened?"

I gave her my theory of Eileen deciding to give her away, probably because she was about to be single again and couldn't raise a child alone.

"It fits. I hate it but it fits."

"I'm so sorry, Ariana. I didn't know how to tell you without causing you anguish."

"You're just the messenger," she said generously, swiping the backs of her hands against her cheeks. "And a good investigator. I wish you weren't so good. I wish it had all never happened. I wish I'd come out here for their twenty-fifth anniversary as I had planned to do. Maybe I could have prevented it all from happening."

"None of this was your fault."

"No. It's just my inheritance."

25

With Ariana's permission, Jack called Joe Fox and told him we had developed some interesting theories that he could hear at his convenience. We were hoping it would be informal, at our home and not at the sheriff's office. He said he was busy that evening but would come over Sunday about eight. Jack said he sounded very calm, that he was not still angry.

Ariana told us she would submit to a DNA test. She might as well find out the truth, not just suspect it. I thought she made a wise decision.

Joe Fox arrived with an unusually large bouquet of flowers for me, and I sensed he was sorry for his unpleasant behavior the last time we had talked. As he and Ariana acknowledged each other, I saw the anger flash in Joe's eyes while she looked at him steadily with defiance. They said nothing and we all sat down.

"Joe, I think we know who killed the Brinkers," I began. I was the designated speaker. Ariana wanted to be present but her dislike of Joe threatened to compromise whatever objectivity she had mustered.

"Well, that's good to hear. I'm glad you've decided to clue me in on it."

"We know some things for sure. The rest isn't yet

proven, but probably can be. I didn't see it till early Saturday morning."

"You didn't see it."

"I finally put it all together," I explained, unhappy at his sarcastic tone.

"OK."

"The Brinkers were murdered by Mrs. Brinker's twin sister."

"You know this." He wasn't giving anything.

"I know there's a twin. I know where she lives." I handed him a copy of my notes from Arnold. "And my theory is that she's Ariana's natural mother."

His eyebrows went up and he turned to look at Ariana. "Did you know about her existence?"

"No."

"Go on," Joe said to me.

"I believe the sister, whose name now is Eileen Foster, hunted the Brinkers from the time Ariana was very young. Eileen gave birth to Ariana and used her twin sister's name on the birth certificate. I'm guessing when she gave birth she was on the verge of a divorce and she felt she couldn't raise a child alone."

"And later she changed her mind," Joe said.

"Yes."

"An old story."

"And a very sad one," Jack interjected.

Joe gave a short nod. "So the Brinkers changed their name, left Portland, and started an odyssey that ended in Oakwood."

I nodded.

"Where she found her sister and brother-in-law and killed them. And we know the rest of the story."

"That's right."

"So tell me about your little trip to Madison, Wisconsin."

Ariana and I had talked about this before his arrival. I had promised that unless I was asked under oath, I would not mention the money. "Ariana and I went to her parents' estate lawyer in New York, where she learned that the house she recalled from her childhood was still owned by her parents, now the estate. We went out there to see it and talk to the Madison attorney."

"Why are you telling me this, Mrs. Brooks? It's not your story to tell. It's Miss Brinker's. Is she unable to speak for herself?"

"Joe," Jack said, "this has been an emotional roller coaster for Ariana. Cut her a little slack. She'll give you a sworn statement at another time. We just want you to know who we think the killer is and where you can find her."

I noticed that when Jack said something, Joe took it more seriously than when I did. It worked this time, too. He nodded in acquiescence.

"So you went out there and this twin followed you. Kind of a long drive to do in a short time."

"Someone was with her—a boyfriend maybe, or a paid helper."

"So they both drove. OK. What did they expect to find out there?"

"Maybe they didn't know," I said. "But Ariana and I were going there together. They must have watched her or my house to see where we were going. And the twin knew about the Madison house. It's why the Brinkers left a number of years ago."

"And the twin kept the sister's license because she looked like the picture and it had the right name on it,

Holly or Rosette or whatever. I've lost track of those names, I have to admit. For this case you need a road map."

"That's right. But the man who was with her didn't look like Ronald Brinker, so they left that license in his wallet."

"So they get to Madison and they go to the house in the middle of the night and break in and find nothing. And when they get back to the car, it's gone. So they know they've done something stupid."

"Right."

"And where do they go from there?"

"I don't know," I said. "Ariana and I came back here." I didn't mention the intervening details: our trip to Portland and then back to Madison, that I flew back from Madison, and that she drove to Chicago and then flew here by herself. "I don't think the twin knows where Ariana lives. Ariana doesn't have a listed phone number and she's moved around a bit herself, going off to college and then to Chicago. So that was a dead end."

"And you think the twin may have gone back to Portland with her accomplice."

"I think there's a good chance of that."

To my surprise, Joe Fox pulled a cell phone out of his pocket and keyed a number he read from his notebook. "Yeah. This is Det. Joe Fox in Oakwood, New York. I'm working with Sergeant Miles on the Brinker case. Uh-huh. Yeah. We have a suspect living in Portland and I'd like her picked up ASAP." He read off Eileen Foster's name, address, and phone number.

We all sat quietly while he continued speaking. He said he wanted her in New York State for questioning. In the meantime, hold her until the paperwork was done. He snapped the phone shut and turned to me.

"Thank you, Mrs. Brooks. Thank you, Miss Brinker." He turned to Jack. "You know what?" he said. "I think you're a saint."

We all laughed.

On Monday, Ariana gave her statement with Arnold at her side. On Tuesday she went into New York to see the estate lawyer. She saw her parents' wills for the first time, and they were quite straightforward, setting out what they owned, where it was located, and that everything they had in the world belonged to their beloved daughter. There was no hint that they were not her natural parents.

Ariana decided to leave her assets untouched for a while and figure out later what to do with them. The lawyer said that would be fine.

Arnold called in the evening to say that he had the dates that Ariana's grandparents died. The grandfather had died first, when Ariana was about four years old, a couple of years after her parents had left Portland for San Diego. I was glad that the facts fit my theory.

We got word that Eileen Foster had been picked up and extradition was in the works. Ariana was conflicted about talking to this woman, who was her nearest biological relative and her most dangerous enemy. The woman had apparently said nothing to the Portland police, and I suspected she would continue that way. There wasn't much she could say that would help her except to make her sister out as a villain who deserved punishment.

Eileen flew east with a police escort a few days later. Ariana had given a blood sample on Monday to check the DNA, which turned out to be unnecessary. The blood type alone indicated Ronald Brinker could not have been her natural father. Although she suspected it, the news unnerved her.

She debated whether she wanted to meet Eileen, or even look at her. I couldn't advise her; it was too personal a decision. Eventually, she decided to do it, just so that she wouldn't torture herself. At her request, I drove up to the jail with her. She said nothing as we drove, her distress visible.

Eileen Foster was sitting at a table in an interrogation room. We looked through a one-way glass and Ariana drew her breath.

"That's my mother," she said. "The hair is different, but the face—it's unbelievable."

I had to agree that the woman at the table was the image of the woman in the recent snapshot Ariana carried.

"You want to talk to her?" Joe Fox asked.

"I don't know."

"Take your time."

"Yes, OK. Let me in there." She was actually holding my hand and she threatened to crush it as she spoke. "I'll go in alone."

"We'll be right here. Just let us know when you want out. You don't have to say anything to her if you don't want to."

I watched as Joe led her to the door, opened it, and let her in. She walked toward the table, then stopped. Eileen looked up, her face angry. Then she seemed to realize whom she was looking at and her face softened. She looked as though she might cry.

Ariana said nothing. She simply stood and inspected the woman sitting in the chair.

Then Eileen said, "I wanted you so much."

Ariana nodded.

"They wouldn't let me have you. They wouldn't let me see you. They acted as though I didn't exist."

Ariana swallowed. I wondered what she would do, what she would say. "They were my parents," she said finally. "Everything they did was in my best interests." Then she turned and went to the door. Joe went around and unlocked it. When she came out, she hugged me and cried.

Joe had told us that there was convincing forensic evidence that could be used against Eileen. A piece of her clothing, a scarf, had been found in the SUV. On it were Eileen's hair, her perfume, and traces of the oil that comes off one's neck. Also, Elaine Brinker's driver's license had been found in Eileen's home. So were the keys to the vehicle and to the apartment in Oakwood.

She had been asked several times to identify her companion, but she said nothing. An attorney had been appointed for her and she showed no sign of wanting to find one of her own.

Having seen Eileen, Ariana told me she now felt a kind of peace. "I think it's over for me," she said. "I wanted to know how I would feel. She's not my mother and she never was. She gave me away to better people, and they gave me their lives and their love."

"Joe said he's releasing the bodies," I said.

"I've decided to bury them here in Oakwood. This was the last place they lived and it's a nice place. I could live here myself."

I smiled. "Maybe you will one day."

"Maybe."

She came to dinner, prepared to fly back to Chicago the next day. While we were sitting around talking in the evening, she said, "That was some wedding my parents had."

"Really?" I said.

"Huge. There was a name orchestra and about four hundred people. It was just amazing."

"How do you know?"

"I found it in the paper. I did what you suggested. It was on microfilm in the library."

"But the papers didn't cover it."

"The one I looked at did. I printed out the article, but it's in the hotel. It had descriptions of the flowers and the orchestra, and it named a lot of the people who were there."

"Something's wrong."

"What do you mean?" Jack asked.

"Jessie checked the papers. She called and said there were no articles."

"Maybe she was too busy to be bothered," Jack said.

I held my breath a moment before saying, "Maybe her husband was Eileen's companion."

There was absolute stillness in the room. Both of them were looking at me.

"How is that possible?" Ariana said. "We saw Nick in Portland the Sunday we arrived from Madison."

"All that means is that he drove to Madison with Eileen on the Friday we flew there. They alternated driving and didn't stop to sleep, so they arrived sometime Saturday. We went to the house Saturday morning and you called his number that afternoon."

"And Jessie said he was on a business trip but would be back the next day." Ariana looked shocked. "Who goes on a business trip on Saturday?"

"Good question," I said. "He flew home on Sunday after they broke into the house, or maybe before. Maybe she did it herself. When she—or they—got back to where the car was parked, it was gone, and she got scared and flew out of town, maybe right back to Portland, where she lives. There's enough time there for everything. That drop of blood in your parents' apartment in Oakwood doesn't match anyone in the case. Maybe it matches Nick."

Ariana looked confused. "How did Eileen find him?"

"The way you did. She looked up Brinkers in the phone book. Remember, Nick never got any money from his grandparents. It went to Aunt Junie. Aunt Junie's still alive and she's living on it, and living very nicely. Her clothes were expensive. Her hair was done by a professional. There may not be much—or any—left for Nick when she dies. Eileen knew your father got an inheritance, or at least she assumed he did. Maybe she promised Nick money if he would help her."

"Good thinking," Jack said.

"They were so nice," Ariana said. "There were so kind to us."

"Maybe he thought you'd lead him to money."

"But he took us to see his mother. What if she had said something about Eileen?"

"She almost did, remember? And when I called back and asked Jessie if she could ask her mother-in-law some questions, Nick called and said Junie had had a setback."

"Which may never have happened."

"Right. We don't even know if Nick asked her any more questions. I'd guess he didn't."

"Looks like we have to call Joe Fox again," Jack said. "This is starting to be a habit."

26

The Portland police brought Nick Brinker in for questioning. I felt terrible for Jessie, although she must have known what was going on if she lied to me about the article in the paper. Still, she was a young wife and mother, and her husband might be charged with a terrible crime.

He admitted that he was Eileen's partner but denied he had done any killing. That, he said, was all Eileen's doing. She had used chloroform on the woman and a gun on the man. He identified the caliber of the gun as the same that forensics said had been used to kill Ronald Brinker. He said Eileen had buried that and the small bottle of chloroform in a cemetery near Oakwood. Eventually, they were dug up with his help. Then a series of test-fired bullets were compared to the bullets taken from Ronald Brinker's body, and a match was made with the suspect gun, a .38 caliber Smith & Wesson Airweight with a one-inch barrel.

After Ariana left town, Jack and I had a little talk about the money she dug up in Madison. I didn't want to talk about it publicly and had told Ariana how I felt.

"Did you see that money?" Jack asked.

"I saw the suitcase and one packet of bills."

"So you only know what was in the suitcase from hearsay?"

I thought about it. "I guess you could say so."

"I don't think you'll have a problem."

When Nick Brinker was extradited to New York State, I asked Joe Fox if I could see him. I went up on a warm day when Eddie was in day camp and Jack at work. Prisons make me nervous, and I was glad to have Joe accompany me to the room where Nick sat waiting for me. Joe had promised us a private talk and I trusted him.

Nick hardly looked like himself. He had lost weight and his face was haggard. Had I seen him on the street, I would not have recognized him.

We had a long talk, most of which was irrelevant to the homicides, but he told me some things that put the last few pieces of the puzzle in place.

"How did you get to know Eileen Foster?" I asked.

"She called me a long time ago—I don't remember when. She knew I was Uncle Ron's nephew and she was curious about the Brinker inheritance. I told her Dad had left Mom his share. I think she gave me a thousand dollars after he died. My sister got that, too."

"Did you know about Ariana?"

"Uh-uh. At least, not at first. I knew Eileen had a grudge, but I figured it had something to do with money. She called me a few months ago and asked if I would help her out. She said there was money and she would split it with me fifty-fifty. I have to tell you, I could have used it. We've had a hard time and whatever it was, even ten thousand, it would have been good to have.

"Eileen said she had located her sister and brother-in-law, and she wanted me along when she went to talk to them. I thought she might be afraid for her safety, although I didn't know why."

"And you came to Oakwood with her?"

"Yeah." He rubbed his hands over his face at that point, and I thought, He must be wishing he'd never taken that trip.

"Tell me what happened, Nick."

"We found them in their apartment. I didn't know Eileen had a gun with her until that day. She'd put it in the suitcase she checked on the plane. She said she was sure they'd never find it and she was right. She threatened them with it and had me tie Uncle Ron up with some plastic things she had. That was when I knew I'd bitten off more than I could chew.

"She asked them where Ariana was and they didn't answer. She got mad, she screamed at them, but they just sat there. Then she asked them for money. She said she'd spare their lives if they gave her money. They just sat there like pieces of wood. I could see Eileen was getting madder and madder. Every second they didn't say anything, she got closer to blowing up. You know, she's not a real stable person. She said something to me—I think she was in a nuthouse for a while."

I cringed at the word. "A mental institution?"

"Yeah, whatever. I can tell you she scared me a couple of times. Maybe they knew that, Uncle Ron and his wife. Maybe that's why they were so scared of her."

That could be yet another reason why they kept running, I thought. "When Eileen demanded money from them, did she mention any special amount?" I asked.

"Nah. She had told me they had a lot of money put away. That's what she wanted. Then she asked me to hold Elaine for a minute, and she put something on Elaine's face. She slid down to the floor and the next thing I knew she was dead. I didn't kill her. I didn't know what was going on."

"I understand," I said, watching him become almost tearful.

"Then she asked Uncle Ron again where the money was. He didn't answer. He kept looking at Elaine lying there on the floor. He was—honest to God—he was in tears. I was too, if you want to know the truth."

"And then what?"

"She shot him." He trembled as though the memory was too much for him. "She pushed the gun right into his chest and shot him, just like that. And they were both dead. We took their jewelry off, we went through their wallets. And when it was about one or two in the morning, we carried them out to the car wrapped in blankets."

Later in the conversation I asked him about the trip to Madison.

"I went home after the—after it happened. Eileen had made a crazy phone call after we emptied the apartment— she had had me shoot her gun into a pillow—and she said someone would find the bodies, and then their daughter would show up and she would get the money from her. With the apartment empty, people would think they had moved, evidence would be gone, and the police would be in a state of confusion."

"Nick," I said, interrupting, "your blood was found in the bedroom in that apartment."

"Oh yeah, the blood. That was Eileen's idea. She said to prick my finger and leave some on the rug to throw the police off. We never thought we'd be found, at least I felt pretty confident."

"Go on with your story. You said Eileen waited around in Oakwood."

"Right. I couldn't wait around, but she did. A couple of weeks later, she called and told me to take the first plane out here. The daughter had arrived.

"It was crazy. We watched this girl. She went to your house. She went to a motel. Then one morning, the two of you went to the airport."

"And you followed."

"Yeah. Eileen drove the SUV. I got out when you and Ariana went to the curbside check-in. I was so close to you, I thought you might have seen me. I heard her say Madison to the baggage guy, and I dashed back to where Eileen was sitting in the car."

"And you drove to Madison."

"Yeah. Eileen said she knew where you were going."

"What did you expect to find in the house?"

"I don't know. Eileen didn't tell me much. We broke into the house, looked around with a flashlight, and got out. There was nothing there. I called Jessie later and she told me Ariana had called, so I flew home. That was it. I never saw Eileen again."

Like so many of the homicides I have looked into in the past several years, this was another sad one, one in which I could understand why the killer did what she did. I could see how she could come to regret the decision to give up her child, made before the child was born, before she had a chance to look at her, to hold her in her arms. And without any difficulty, I could see the Brinkers' side just as clearly. They took possession of their daughter when she was only a few days old and they considered her theirs, as she truly was. The demand to give her up must have been so shocking, so frightening, that they could think of only one response.

Having observed similar cases in the news, I would guess that had they attempted to mediate, they might well have had to share their child. They wanted her for their own. And they died for it.

Ariana had a simple funeral and burial for her parents. Jack took the morning off and we went together. I was pleased to see Det. Joe Fox put in an appearance. When it was over, Ariana returned to the hotel and left for Chicago later in the day.

She sent a postcard from Chicago about a month later saying she was fine. And later in the summer she sent another one from Guatemala. She sounded very happy.

But the most unexpected thing happened in the fall. Eddie went back to school, this time in the first grade. He was very excited, as we all were, and he began to read soon after the beginning of the semester.

As it was fall, I did the seasonal change of clothes, putting away the shorts and bathing trunks and short-sleeved shirts and replacing them with cool-weather clothes. I asked Eddie to pull out the shoes and stored items in the corner of his closet so I could get rid of the accumulated dust. He went inside and came out with an armful of things. We set them on the bedroom floor, and I started through them to decide which we would give away and which we would keep for another season.

"What's this?" I asked, coming on a small package wrapped in brown paper and kept together with several rubber bands.

"I don't know. It was on the floor. Look. Here's my baseball I couldn't find."

"Well, put it where you'll have it in the spring." I removed rubber band after rubber band, finally opening the brown bag. I pulled out a small packet, also rubber-banded. And my heart stopped.

It was a stack of hundred-dollar bills with a note.

"This is for Eddie's college education." Not another word.

I recalled that Ariana had gone up to put Eddie to bed one night and she had taken the straw bag upstairs with her. No other explanation made sense.

"What is it?" Eddie asked.

"Nothing important. Let's go through the shoes." My heart pounding, I rewrapped the bills in the bag. I would show them to Jack tonight.

I called the Chicago phone number but it was disconnected. I tried Guatemala, but that, too, was out of service. I tried information, but there was no Ariana Brinker in Chicago or Madison. Eventually, I put the packet in our safe-deposit box along with our insurance policies. It seemed an appropriate place.

I haven't heard from Ariana since the last postcard. She must be having a good time.